Sam, a novel

Other Books By Charlotte Lewis

The Oregon Trail Series:
    Becky

    Rebecca

    Anna

    Amanda

Mystery & Suspense Stories
    Chris

    Eleanor

    Bethany

    The House

    Eve

Sam, a novel

Thanks, Richard!
Charlotte Lewis

Charlotte Lewis

Copyright © 2010 by Charlotte Lewis.

ISBN: Softcover   978-1-4568-0048-2
         Ebook   978-1-4568-0049-9

All rights reserved. No part of this book may be reproduced or transmitted in any form or by any means, electronic or mechanical, including photocopying, recording, or by any information storage and retrieval system, without permission in writing from the copyright owner.

This is a work of fiction. Names, characters, places and incidents either are the product of the author's imagination or are used fictitiously, and any resemblance to any actual persons, living or dead, events, or locales is entirely coincidental.

This book was printed in the United States of America.

To order additional copies of this book, contact:
Xlibris Corporation
1-888-795-4274
www.Xlibris.com
Orders@Xlibris.com
88495

Dedication

For my son and his dog.

Prologue

The television people have gone, finally. Cameras, lights, a reporter and a camera person—all crowded into my living room this afternoon. You could believe no one around here had ever lived to 101 before.

I half expected this hubbub last year when I turned one hundred. But George Burns' birthday was a couple months before mine and, by the time my birthday rolled around, old George had croaked over. So, my 100th birthday was either overlooked or just plain overshadowed. Ego requires me to believe it was overshadowed by the death of a very large named person.

Frankly, I didn't mind too much about that. I was feeling my age, almost, last year. But somehow this year I got a second wind and was ready for television. Truth be told, I would have been a bit deflated if they had skipped over me a second time. Nothing major happened newswise before my birthday this year.

One hundred one years! My, what a long time that is. If I can last another four years I can say I lived in three different centuries. That makes the years sound even longer, doesn't it? Well, I'll have to think about that awhile. I have come from horse and buggy to walking on the moon. The enormous history of the last hundred years is phenomenal.

But I'll have to think about that later. I have much else to ponder this evening. The reporter asked me if there was any one particular incident or person in my 101 years that stood out in my memory. Imagine! 101 years and he's asking for one single memory. Perhaps he believes I am too old to remember anything. And because of the progress of the last century, you'd think he'd come up with a better question. One thing, indeed. But I am sure I didn't even hesitate when I told him the one person I most vividly recalled was a young man named Samuel Christian Olenger. The TV fellow asked, "Why is that, Mrs. Willoughby? What makes him so special?"

"How much time do you have, young man?" I was trying to be polite. "The story of young Sam Olenger is a long one for no longer than he lived."

"Was he a local here in Cayucos, Mrs. Willoughby?"

I did hesitate there though I'm not sure why. Young Sam lived here all but two days of his life. The first two days of his life. But whether or not he was local—well, I just couldn't say. There was always something about that boy that made me wonder truly who he was and where he came from.

Oh, I know who came around saying she was his mother. But somehow, I never quite believed it. Maybe I didn't want to believe. I am not sure—not even after all these years. But there was always something about Young Sam that made one wonder if perhaps he wasn't a little bit like Clark Kent—and not of this world. Okay, Clark Kent is a fictional character but there were times I used to wonder if Young Sam wasn't a bit fictional himself.

The reporter was tapping his pencil on his clipboard so I figured I'd better hurry up and answer his question before he changed his mind. "He lived here, in this very house, his entire life. He was a hero when the cannery caught fire in 1944; saved the owner and several of the young ladies who worked the number four canning line. Yes, he was a local."

The TV fellow made a couple of scribbles in his notebook. "You say he lived in this house?"

"Yes, he and his two uncles. I was their housekeeper for more than twenty-five years. They left the house to me when they passed on."

I think the television fellow didn't hear a good story in that and he went on to a few of the usual questions, the ones no one listens to the answers. To what do I attribute my long life . . . special diet, exercise, the ocean air? Stupid questions that no one hears the answers.

I knew if I told him what I really think has kept me going all these years, the young fellow would snort and shake his head. He'd think "Poor, old, delusional woman." So I just told him, "No, nothing special. I've just led a charmed life, I guess."

And in a way, that may be true. Truth be told, I think it was Young Sam that gave me the ability to live on and on. I wish the television folk would have had time to hear the whole story. And now, as he has dredged up the memories, I guess I'll be spending the rest of the evening recalling Young Sam and the Cayucos of long ago all by myself.

Ah! Those were the days. I remember them as if they were just last week.

Chapter One

Ah! Those were the days. I remember them as if they were just last week. The reporter asked about one incident or one person. The biggest problem with memories is that one always brings another. You can't jump into the middle of your life and pull up one remembrance without disturbing several others. But the one person that stands out in my memory is Samuel Christian Olenger. Young Sam. He was a darling baby, an inquisitive toddler, a daring boy—blond, blue-eyed and as friendly as anyone could ever be.

When I think of Young Sam, I end up at the very beginning. Nowadays that is nearly a hundred years ago. It seems now that I've had time to think about it, that my entire life led up to knowing and caring for Young Sam It takes a while to 'get' to Young Sam this way but everything that happened before him is an important part of the memory.

I was born right here in Cayucos—over on Ocean Street. I lived here all my life. My family was never into traveling a lot so, other than the coast of Central California, I don't know a lot about the world that I haven't gleaned from newspapers, radio and television. And I was twelve or 13 before I heard a radio.

As a young girl, my family went to San Francisco. We visited all the tourist spots including museums, the waterfront and such. In one of the museums I saw a painting of an Indian on horseback on a cliff. Or maybe it was a cowboy, but I wanted to be that person. Of course, we didn't own a horse but I would climb the cliffs above our house in Cayucos and pretend I was on horseback. The brisk, often cold, winds off the ocean would blow my braids apart and chap my face. It didn't take long to decide there had to be better things to be. I was eight or nine at that time.

Boys never seemed to interest me. Perhaps it was the lack of selection in Cayucos rather than a lack of interest. I was a typical young girl of the time. We didn't have lofty aspirations much back then because we just didn't know much about the outside world. Newspapers weren't delivered to your front door and there was no television. The average girl aspired to be her Mother. Well, perhaps not her Mother, but to be a married woman with a house of her own. No one thought of becoming a movie star or famous singer or dancer—those things were not of our world then. I am not sure we even used the word career back then; at least, not in relation to ourselves. Girls wanted to be married and live happily ever after.

At fifteen, I was about five feet tall, had green eyes and, according to my father, was a bit of a spitfire. The other girls wore their hair in buns but I had seen real hair styles when we were in San Francisco and never forgot them. By the time I was out of braids I wore my long sandy red hair in a chignon. I finished high school at sixteen. Most of my friends got married within the next year or so. I hadn't found the "right" person though.

At seventeen I was not married but had a paying job. This was quite unusual back then. There wasn't enough money to go away to college and I believe I wouldn't have gone even if there had been as I saw no need for more education. My father worked at the local wharf and heard the owner, Mr. Sam Olenger, comment he needed to hire a person for the office who could write and do sums well. Father insisted I go to the Wharf with him the next morning and speak to Mr. Sam. Father knew our family would be moving from the area soon but he also knew I wanted to stay. A paying job was the only solution. I applied and was immediately hired. My family moved from Cayucos to Morro Bay shortly after. I rented a room from Mrs. Spenser, a neighbor on Ocean Street, who took in boarders for a small fee. Morro Bay is just down the coast a bit, not a thousand miles away and staying connected with my family would not be a problem.

My position at the Olenger Wharf and Cannery was secretary/bookkeeper. The pay was good for the time and my gender. I loved my job. The Olengers, Sam and Daisy, were like second parents to me, especially at holidays and my birthday, though I would go to Morro Bay for Christmas and some other times of the year to spend time with my family. Mr. Olenger always gave me a nice Christmas gift and a year-end bonus if the year had been good at the Wharf. Daisy frequently sent cookies or other treats to me. She always remembered my birthday.

Sam and Daisy had two boys, Theodore and Woodrow. Ted, Woody and I went to school at the same time though they were younger than me. That's the nice thing about small town schools—all the older kids are in one classroom. We all knew one another well. Ted and Woody were like two peas in a pod. They were a year and a half apart in age but strangers frequently took them for twins. If they had been older than me, I might have been more interested in boys. Back in those days girls weren't interested in younger boys. Ted was the smarter of the two, book-wise, but Woody had the people smarts. He could charm even Old Mrs. Munro into smiling. (She didn't like boys or girls for that matter and chased us away from her yard constantly.) Ted and Woody both were tall, white blond hair and rather good looking. Woody had hazel eyes and Ted had green eyes. Their eyes were the only real difference in their appearance.

The Olenger boys thought it was great their Dad hired me. They had dropped out of school the year I graduated. They were fifteen and sixteen. I thought it was a shame they felt they didn't need more schooling to work at the Wharf. It was obvious at the time that Mr. Olenger needed help as the cannery part of the business was picking up in 1913. The cannery line had been added to the Wharf a few years before as a sort of experiment and had gone well. Fishing boats could now come into Cayucos instead of going down the coast to Morrow Bay or Monterey.

A week before my 19th birthday in April 1915, I met Mr. Willoughby. He was first mate on the Mary Catherine, a fishing trawler that docked regularly at the Olenger Wharf. That's what the Wharf was called back then. As secretary I didn't get out of the office too often, but this day Mr. Olenger asked me to take a receipt for dockage payment to the captain of the Mary Catherine. She was docked and had been unloaded. However, the captain had gone ashore and the only person of authority on board at that time was the first mate, Mr. Willoughby.

Over the years, since then, I have heard songs about how the heart beats, the strings pling, the blood surges when you meet your true love. I hadn't heard such songs before then. But meeting Mr. Willoughby—well, my heart thumped so loudly it is a wonder he didn't hear it. I know that I flushed a deep red when he spoke to me as I could feel the warmth surge into my face. Yes, I was nearly overwhelmed. Mr. Willoughby was tall, more than six feet. He had a shock of luxuriant black hair that waved its way over his collar. His eyes were as blue as the ocean itself. Or maybe as blue as the sky on a perfect summer day. He wore a moustache, handsomely trimmed. His hands were large but had a kind of gentle look about them. He appeared to be old though, perhaps thirty. Even so, I had never met a man who impressed me so.

Mr. Willoughby had been first mate on the Mary Catherine for several years and I cannot imagine how I missed him each time the ship docked before. There are times I think that Mr. Olenger knew the captain was ashore. Mr. Olenger was always telling me I should find a good man, marry and settle down. The Mary Catherine was going to have several repairs made while in port this trip and would be tied up at the Wharf for at least two weeks.

Mr. Willoughby was most proper and polite when I gave him the paperwork that day. By afternoon he had inquired as to my name, marital status and age . . . . he didn't ask me, he asked Ted and Woody. They came into the office to tease me as I cleared my desk for the day. I was flattered, of course. Truth be told, the fact he had inquired caused my heart to race again.

Evidently Mr. Willoughby realized I had no family in town so he went to Mr. Olenger to ask permission to call on me. Mr. Olenger was more excited than I had ever seen him the next morning when I arrived at work. He inquired whether I would be interested in having Mr. Willoughby, first mate of the Mary Catherine, call on me.

Would I? It had been love at first sight for us both. Don't believe those people who tell you that no such thing exists. It does, and it did.

A week after my birthday, we were married. Mr. and Mrs. Olenger gave us a very nice party after the wedding. Everyone in town was invited to both the wedding and the party. The Mary Catherine sailed the next day.

Under usual circumstance I would have left my employment with the Wharf. That's pretty much how things were done. But Mr. Olenger said that because Mr. Willoughby was a seafaring man and would be gone for weeks at a time, I could stay on until we decided to start a family. At that time, I could tender my notice. I thought that was right considerate of him. The marriage had happened so quickly I had no time to make other living arrangements. Mr. Willoughby figured I had a room and he wasn't going to be around, so why worry? So I continued on in my little rented room.

The Mary Catherine would be in port for two or three days every four or five weeks. As we were legally married, Mrs. Spenser had no problem with Mr. Willoughby staying with me those few days.

A year passed. In that year we had spent 25 days together. Mr. Willoughby was a very kind man and we enjoyed one other very much. Finally, the Mary Catherine would be in port for annual repairs—much as when we first met. Mr. Willoughby bought a small house for us a few blocks from the Wharf. We had nearly a week to furnish it before the Mary Catherine left port. When he sailed, Mr. Willoughby left me a sizeable bank account so I could move from Mrs. Spenser's and into the house. Though the furniture was in place, there were dishes to buy, linens, pots, pans and such. By the next time the Mary Catherine docked, I had transformed the little house into a comfortable home.

Mr. Willoughby thought it was time to start a family. My advancing age was a major concern. I was over twenty by then. He would still be gone regularly but, now that we had a home of our own, he felt the time was right. I agreed.

That fall I became pregnant and gave Mr. Olenger my notice. He was happy for me even though he had a terrible time finding another suitable secretary. He had become quite used to me by then, you see. I had been there over three years.

Times were so different then. These young women who run around today with their bellies stuck out to Cleveland have no idea what it was like in 1917 to be pregnant. You stayed home—or visited discreetly with your women friends and your family. The baby was due close to our second anniversary. Mr. Willoughby asked my mother if she could come from Morro Bay to stay with me the last month. He would go out with the Mary Catherine in late February but would stay ashore when she went out again in April so he would be home for the birthing. His captain would expect him back on board when the ship sailed at the end of May. My mother was agreeable to his plan and came in early March.

But things didn't happen the way Mr. Willoughby had so carefully planned. A storm of extreme nature overtook the Mary Catherine on March 16th, capsized her, took the ship, cargo and the crew. All on board perished.

I was nearing my ninth month. Mother was with me when the news of the disaster was delivered to the house. I went into labor and the baby, a little boy, was stillborn. The doctor suggested I return home with my mother and stay with her in Morro Bay for a few weeks. He thought things might look better when I returned. Mr. Olenger arranged for the baby's funeral. I hadn't even thought of that. He was so small. I named him Homer after his father. The local priest insisted on baptizing the baby before he was buried. That single act broke my heart almost more than the baby's death, I think. I couldn't believe that any religion could believe an innocent baby, who had never taken a single breath, would be denied entry into heaven. Needless to say, I was not then and am not now a Catholic.

Two weeks after I returned from my mother's home, Mrs. Olenger took ill. The doctors couldn't seem to pin down her problem. Mr. Olenger took her to San Luis Obispo to see several specialists. None had an answer. She needed round-the-clock care; at least 24-hour a day observation. Mr. Olenger came to my little house, his hat in his hand. "Agnes, would you be able to stay with Mrs. Olenger during the day. She doesn't require a lot of care but I can't leave her alone."

I hesitated just a moment. It wasn't that I couldn't do it. But I was still grieving the loss of Mr. Willoughby and my baby son. I hesitated only because I was surprised he would come to me in this time of my grief.

"Agnes, I'll pay you."

That took me aback. I hadn't hesitated because I was thinking of monetary gain. I felt terrible thinking he might be thinking that I was thinking of what would be in it for me.

"Mr. Olenger, I don't how good I'd be. I am still in mourning. I wouldn't want to pull Daisy into depression because I am depressed."

He put his arm around my shoulders. "Agnes, perhaps this will help you as well as Daisy. Please, think about it."

"What exactly would my duties be, Mr. Olenger?"

He outlined the dressing and feeding that Mrs. Olenger could no longer do for herself. But mainly, he said, the job would be to keep her comfortable.

"That's all?"

Mr. Olenger looked at me in surprise. "What else would there be?"

"Don't you need someone to keep the house running. Maybe make supper, do the laundry. Mrs. Olenger isn't able to do that."

"Well, no, she isn't. But I didn't want to burden you with too much. Just caring for Daisy is enough."

I thought about it for a moment. He evidently thought I was going to say no.

"Agnes, I'll pay you five dollars a week."

My head snapped up. Five dollars a week was more than he paid me when I worked for him at the Wharf. "Mr. Olenger, for that kind of money, I would have to take care of the house as well."

A tear rolled down his cheek. I was amazed. I'd never seen a grown many cry before. "If you are serious, Agnes, when can you start?"

The next morning I arrived at the Olenger house just before 7am. Mr. Olenger was pleased that I arrived early enough that he could be at work when the office opened for daily business.

And thus began my career as housekeeper for the Olengers. Of course, at the time, I didn't realize it was going to be a long-term arrangement.

Mrs. Olenger's doctor came every day. Some days he was encouraged but most days he was very dour when he left. All he would say was, "Keep doing whatever it is that you're doing, Mrs. Willoughby. Daisy is comfortable and doing as well as can be expected."

Daisy Olenger died the following July. It had been a long arduous year for us all. The death certificate said she died of ovarian cancer. Unfortunately, in those days, I guess that was one of those diseases diagnosed only in autopsy. I grieved her death as if she had been my own mother. I had become very close to her in that year and loved her very much. Daisy Olenger had been a good friend and wonderful lady.

Chapter Two

After Daisy Olenger died, I thought I would be out of a job. I wasn't too concerned as I did have a house that was paid for and there was a bit of money in the bank. I had saved nearly every penny Mr. Olenger paid me to care for Daisy plus the money from Mr. Willoughby. I would comfortable for a long time.

Then Mr. Olenger asked if I would stay on as he still needed a cook and housekeeper. I could not say no—the job would be much easier without having to care for Mrs. Olenger—and it would give me a reason to get up every morning.

Mr. Olenger and the boys were scattered people after Daisy's death. She had been the glue that kept the family together. Even when she was so ill, she had been their mainstay, their anchor. They had trouble functioning without her. They had come to rely on me for so much while she was ill and that dependency continued after. But they had no focus other than the Wharf.

My routine changed a bit. I didn't go to the house until afternoon, except on wash day. The men made their own breakfast. I would tidy the kitchen and clean the rest of the house after I arrived each afternoon. Before leaving each day, I prepared supper. It was always ready at 5:30 and I stayed until then—to put supper on the table. If they were going to be late they would call. Central rang two shorts and a long for the Olenger house. On those days, I'd put dinner in the oven and go home at 5:30. This was a rare occurrence however.

Sometime in late 1919 Mr. Olenger added my name to his charge account at the community grocery. Soon I was doing all of the shopping as well as the housekeeping. He said it was just easier for him not to worry about buying groceries. What did he know about it anyhow—he just followed a list I had prepared so why shouldn't I do the shopping? I was flattered he would put so much trust in me. The grocer confided in me that he had suggested the change as it appeared Mr. Olenger had no idea what to buy at times even with my list and someone would have to assist him with his shopping.

Before 1919 had ended it was apparent that Mr. Olenger was not at all well. He went to the doctor only when the boys insisted. He said there was nothing wrong with him but I watched his health decline steadily. By March 1920 Mr. Olenger was not much more than a walking skeleton. His stamina was gone. Ted confided that his father could barely make the short walk to the Wharf without sitting and resting once or twice. The boys had discreetly made several small wooden benches to place along the beach path from house to wharf so Mr. Olenger could rest along the way. I know he was aware the benches had been made for his use but he went along with the idea that anyone could sit and watch the ocean if one so desired while out walking. Though what they would be doing on that path would be a question.

Woody continually asked his father what the doctor had to say about his condition. Mr. Olenger insisted the doctor couldn't find anything wrong. He was eating well but it was not evident. He was skin and bones; his skin was almost translucent. Ted took off one afternoon to make the trip to talk with the doctor alone. The doctor said he thought, quite frankly, that Mr. Olenger had no interest in living. He was dying slowly from melancholy. There seemed no medical explanation. Ted said that seemed so strange—the doctor said there was absolutely nothing he could do. Mr. Olenger was the only one that could make any difference and that didn't seem too likely.

Two years, almost to the anniversary date of Mrs. Olenger's death, Mr. Olenger died. He was at his desk at the Wharf. Ted went in to ask him if he wanted to go home for dinner. Ted and Woody had been suggesting he eat dinner at home, instead of packing a lunch, thinking he might eat more. I always had something that could be prepared in a few minutes. But Mr. Olenger was dead. The doctor came immediately though there was nothing he could do. The old man had just stopped breathing. The whole town went into mourning. Some people were concerned that the Wharf would close but Ted and Woody assured everyone things would go on as usual. The will was read the following week. Everything was left to the boys except for a small stipend for me for, what his will termed, devoted service.

There was much more to the estate than the boys had expected. Besides the anticipated checking and savings accounts there was a very large amount of money in investments. The real estate holdings included the Wharf and the ten acres around it; the house and the two acres it stood on and several other pieces of property in town. Some of the property was rental property and there was income realized from that. Also there were vacant lots that Mr. Olenger had gathered up over the years that comprised a large portion of the town.

The safety deposit box contained several notes showing that Mr. Olenger had loaned money to many townspeople, mostly small business men. They had all given him an IOU—no other collateral. One of the first things Ted and Woody did was to take all loan notes home where they poured over them at the kitchen table. The total amount was barely more than twenty thousand dollars—but in 1920 that was big money. They spent several hours going over the other items from the safe deposit box—a box they hadn't even known existed before their father's death. When they had reviewed everything quite thoroughly, they asked me if I could stay for supper the next night and help them with some writing afterwards. I said I could do that. After supper that next night, the brothers brought out a pad of white paper, a box of envelopes and the IOUs. One by one we went through them. A note for each was written which said "Enclosed please find the IOU you gave to our father, Samuel Olenger—on whatever date the Note was dated in the amount of whatever it was. We believe our father would want this debt erased and your IOU returned to you. It is our hope that in return you will be willing to help someone else in his time of need." I cried as I wrote out the nineteen notes. Both boys signed them after I had finished. They folded the original IOU into the note, put it into an envelope and I addressed them with the name only.

Before the office opened at the Wharf the next morning, the boys took the notes and hand-delivered them to their father's former debtors. I felt such pride at that moment. I am sure Sam and Daisy were looking down from somewhere pleased with what was happening. Some of the IOUs were more than ten years old. As Mr. Olenger had never pursued collection, I am sure he hadn't intended to try to collect. All nineteen were business people—some of the businesses were growing in size, some were static, but all were still in business. Possibly because of the money they had borrowed from Sam Olenger.

Ted and Woody asked if I could stay on as housekeeper as they knew little, if anything, about cleaning, washing or cooking. I said of course I would stay. They gave me a raise. I was now making ten dollars a week. It was comforting to see my savings account grow. There weren't too many things I needed and so could save most of my earnings.

In 1921, the boys incorporated the Wharf. It's official name was the TWO Wharf and Cannery, Inc. I asked what the TWO stood for. They were quite amazed that I didn't figure that one out immediately . . . Theodore & Woodrow Olenger. Of course!!

Over the next several months I found drawings scattered on the kitchen table nearly every afternoon when I came. After the drawings more or less disappeared there were lists—several lists with numbers, dollar amounts and odd notes.

The drawings were to add two new canning lines to the cannery and to expand the actual wharf further out into the Pacific Ocean so larger fishing ships could dock and unload. When the plans were finalized and made known, the town went crazy. Already the largest employer, the Wharf would also be the largest business in Cayucos. Several townspeople were hired by the contactors doing the expansion work. Nearly every contract contained a contingency that required hiring as many locals as possible to complete the contract. Strangely, as least to me, it seemed Sam Olenger's death benefitted the town greatly.

The two boys put renewed energy into the cannery and it was soon well known up and down the California coast line. Several people thought it rivaled anything standing on Cannery Row in Monterey. And it was definitely larger than anything operating in Morro Bay. At the time, the Olenger boys were 22 and 23 years old.

The new cannery lines, in a new building wing, took less than three months to complete. The old canning line was moved to the new building. A new employee room was completed where the old canning line had been—immediately behind the office.

New, modern equipment was in place and eighty people were hired to work it. Everything was set up so that two shifts could work six days a week. Additionally, the whole complex was electrified. Boats were docking daily—the long dock was a true maritime marvel It was a great pride for the entire town. A college educated, male accountant was added to the staff.

The cannery and wharf prospered as did the town. The work shift whistle at 7am and 3pm soon became the time-keeper for the town. The presence of the wharf was very prominent. We all settled into a nice comfortable routine. Comfort and routine both ended shortly after 6:30a am on the morning of July 6, 1923.

I was sitting at my breakfast table enjoying a second cup of coffee when my telephone rang. Three shorts. It was Central herself. "Agnes, Woody Olenger would like you to come down to the office as soon as you can."

"Did he say why?" It's unusual for me go to the office anymore. I see the boys in the evening at supper time.

"No, but it must be important. He called Dr. Johnson over in San Luis Obispo before he asked me to call you."

"Thank you, Central. I'll get right down there."

I figured it couldn't be a work injury. The shift whistle hadn't blown yet. I hurried and dressed and walked to the office. I got there just as many of the workers were arriving for their shift. I went directly to the office. It was empty so I knocked on the door to Woody's office. The two brothers stood there looking at a produce crate sitting on Woody's desk. It was the type of crate used by lettuce growers all up and down the state. But the crate's content was what the boys were interested in. They both were leaning on their hands gazing into the crate.

It was a baby.

"Please close the door, Agnes. We want to keep this under wraps for a bit. That's why we just left a message for you with Central. You know she listens in on every call when it's not busy."

"What did you tell Dr. Johnson?"

Ted laughed, "I knew Central would tell you we called him. We just told him that we had sort of "an emergency" at the cannery and could he make it down some time this morning."

"Sort of emergency is right." I picked up the infant and unwrapped it. "This child is very new. I mean, two or three days old only." I peeked into the diaper. "It's a boy."

"Who do you suppose would leave a baby boy on the office doorstep?"

We three stood there trying to think if anyone in town was expecting but came up with no name. The secretary arrived in the outer office just as the whistle blew. Woody went out and told her that he was expecting Dr. Johnson this morning and to please send him up to the house when he arrived. She didn't ask why and I am not sure what Woody would have told her if she had. I asked, "Is there a note with this child?"

The brothers shook their heads. I held the baby and they took everything out of the crate. No note. A bottle filled with milk; one clean diaper and the blanket padding the bottom of the crate. That, and the clothes and blanket he was wrapped in, was everything. No note.

Ted put everything back into the crate and said, "I'm going to take him up to the house, Agnes. I am hoping you'll be able to stay at least until Dr. Johnson arrives."

"What exactly do you want him to do when he gets here?" I rearranged the baby in the crate.

"I'm hoping he may have an idea whose child it is. His practice pretty well covers the area around here. And I'd like him to check the baby to be sure he's okay. Maybe he can give us an idea what to do with him."

That sounded like a pretty tall order for any doctor but, at the same time, he was the doctor that delivered most of the babies in the county. The child looked all right to me. He had the prescribed number of fingers and toes; big blue eyes, peach fuzz hair. He definitely looked like a normal new born. His little hand found my forefinger and gripped it tightly. My heart was beating rather quickly. Memories of another baby boy flashed through my mind; one that had not lived to see the light of day. I followed Ted out the door and to the Olenger house. Woody stayed behind to start the day at the cannery and to direct the doctor to the house. I wondered what he'd tell the secretary and then realized he probably had no intention of telling her anything. How often do you go to work and find a baby in a wooden crate on your office doorstep?

Chapter Three

Dr. Johnson arrived at the house before 8. He was greatly relieved to find that the emergency was a baby. At first, he thought it was funny. Who would leave a baby on the doorstep of a cannery? I agreed it was unusual but, regardless, we had a baby to worry about. He had no patients who were due or past due so he believed the baby was not local. The baby was full term. That raised the question of how did he get here? Cayucos is a small town on a major highway but why would someone select a business as a place to desert a baby? Unless they knew the owners. Both Ted and Woody were sure they did not know anyone who was expecting. We had discussed that at the office before I brought the baby to the house. They were doubtful that anyone they knew would desert a child on a doorstep but would come to the house if they wanted help. We rationalized that when you get off the highway, if you were headed south, probably the cannery would be the first building you'd see. The Olenger house was actually closer to the highway but the cannery is a more imposing structure. The child must have been left during the night. If he had been left at a residence, the people of the house may have heard. No one would hear anything at a closed business. It would be a sure thing he'd be found early the next morning. So the location may have been one of convenience assuring more secrecy than going further into town. This was pure presumption. We found out years later, the person who left the baby had come from the south and driven through the town. The cannery appears to be the last building in Cayucos. All that aside, we still had a child to be cared for.

The doctor proclaimed the baby healthy, probably two days old, close to eight pounds in weight and male. He asked Ted what he planned to do with the child. Would he turn the baby over to the authorities? Ted asked what they would do with him and the doctor said probably end him to the orphanage at Atasadero. Ted looked shocked. I said, "It would be a shame to put an infant into an institution like that. He'd get no love, no special care."

"What else would you do with him, Agnes?" Dr. Johnson was putting all his instruments back into his little black bag. "Do you want to keep him yourself?"

Now it was my turn to look shocked. That thought had never entered my mind and I told him so. You have to understand; there was no welfare system as there is today. No foster care system. That baby would be locked away in an orphanage until he was eighteen and turned loose with a set of clothes and ten dollars in his pocket. He may be trained to do some menial job but he'd never know the love of a family. Orphanages were pretty dismal places back in the 20s. Even more so than now. But even so, I had absolutely no desire to take the child to raise myself.

Ted said, "I'd like to keep him but I don't know how we could manage that." He looked at me as if to ask me to say don't worry, I'll take care of him for you. But I couldn't say that. I had never had a living child and honestly couldn't see the benefit of having one; especially one that had no name, no background, no family. No, I couldn't tell Ted I'd care for the baby.

Woody came in just then and agreed with Ted that he'd like to raise the boy but the how was the question. Then I remembered my brother's daughter, Patricia. Patricia was fifteen, tired of school and had been keeping some pretty shady company of late. My brother threatened to send her to a nunnery almost daily. He was at his wits' end. The girl was intelligent enough; she just had no ambition. Maybe what she needed was a project that required some effort.

"Perhaps my niece could be of some help. She could live here and take care of the house and tend to the baby."

Ted and Woody looked at me like I was crazy. The doctor said that a nanny would certainly solve their problem.

Ted said, "What do you mean, take care of the house and the baby? Wouldn't you be coming in anymore?"

"I could still come and do your laundry and cook your supper but she could do the menial day to day things and watch the baby at the same time. We could call her and ask if she'd be interested."

Dr. Johnson said he had to get back to his office. There was probably already a line of patients waiting. The boys should let him know what they decided. If they decided not to keep the child, he'd make arrangements to send him to Atasadero. Ted picked up the baby and cooed at him. Woody pushed the blanket aside so he could see the bright blue eyes that seemed to be taking in everything that was going on. Such a touching tableau, I thought to myself. These guys would make good parents.

I cranked the phone and asked Central to ring my brother's house. When Patricia was finally on the line I said, "Patty, this is Aunt Agnes. Could you run up to the Olenger house? I have something I'd like to speak to you about. It's important so try not to take too long to get here."

Patricia moaned and groaned a bit—as teenagers are want to do. "Oh, Aunt Agnes, couldn't I come up this afternoon?" I assured her she could not; she was to come as soon as possible.

Poor Central must have been going crazy with curiosity by this time. But the minute she knew we had a baby, the whole town would know. Central was an old maid of about 35. The town switchboard was actually set up in her spare bedroom. Ah, how things have changed!

Patricia showed up an hour later. When Woody put the proposition to her, she jumped at it. It would get her out of her father's house, give her a bit of pocket money and she'd have Sundays off. She agreed to start the next morning. As I had expected, she held the baby and rocked him, talking to him the whole while. His blue eyes tried to follow her movements—he was as enthralled with her as she with him. For a few minutes I thought she might agree to spend the rest of the day but she said she had things to do and would be back first thing in the morning.

Woody said he'd stay home the rest of the day if someone would tell him what to do and when to do it. Then he added, "I'll stay with the baby if someone will buy whatever it requires to care for a newborn." It was rather comical at the time. So Woody drew Baby duty and I went into town to purchase milk, diapers and all the shirts, gowns, blankets and such that a baby needs. The clerk at the mercantile asked if I was expecting and I glared at him. "Indeed not!"

I couldn't believe that he had cheek to ask. He should have been grateful for such a large purchase. Finally, I told him we had unexpected company and they didn't have supplies. At the time I felt I was lying to him but thinking on it on the way home, I realized it was actually the truth.

Back at the Olenger's, I bathed the baby and dressed him in a shirt and gown. He was trying to coo. I wondered if all babies were that alert. In truth, this was the first child I'd come this close to even though I was 27 years old.

I showed Woody how to fasten a diaper and test a bottle for temperature before I left for home. I told him I would be back in the afternoon to clean and make supper, as always. It had been quite a morning. And it certainly wasn't routine.

When I returned later in the day Woody and the baby were both asleep on the divan. Once Woody realized I was there, he put the baby back in his crate and suggested perhaps he should get back to the Wharf. I smiled to myself and told him to go.

Patricia showed up the next morning at the Olenger house at 7am. Woody had already left for the Wharf leaving Ted on Baby duty. Patricia couldn't believe someone could just drop off a baby and leave him all alone in the middle of the night. When I came at 3, I found she hadn't done breakfast dishes or so much as dusted. She said she had forgotten she was supposed to do something more than hold the baby and talk to him. I said I'd forgive her this one time but impressed on her that when I came the next day I expected the house to be clean, including the breakfast dishes.

Supper was ready to be put on the table when Ted and Woody got home that second day. They asked Patricia and me to stay for supper; they wanted to discuss the baby. Fortunately I had made a roast with vegetables and there was plenty. However, there would be no stew later in the week.

They have decided they definitely want to keep the baby. But that means the child has to have a name. They wanted our opinion. Did we think it would be appropriate if they named the baby after their father? Samuel Christian Olenger. We thought it would be appropriate—and nice.

And so, on July 7th, the baby was named.

Ted said that he would call the doctor the next morning to see what had to be done next. Good question—what sort of legal things have to be done to keep a foundling child?

Chapter Four

Ted notified Dr. Johnson who said he'd make arrangements to get some sort of documentation for Young Sam. He said, "Eventually you're going to want to send him to school or something and he'll need proof he was born."

We all thought that was funny. Even the doctor laughed at his little joke. I don't know what he did or how he did it but something came in the mail from the County Recorder a few weeks later that concerned Young Sam. Ted said, "It's something like a substitute birth certificate. His name, date of birth and my and Woody's names. I can't imagine when he'll ever need it but its' good to have, I guess."

And so, once again, we fell into a comfortable routine.

Mondays I went to the house mid-morning to do the laundry. We didn't have the automatic washers and dryers of today. The Olengers had a new GE wringer washer. It was top of line for the time and very efficient. Old Sam had strung a half dozen drying lines for Daisy in the back yard. From time to time I'd have to ask one of the boys to tighten the lines but they were good and sturdy. I could hang all the day's wash without having to wait for some to dry. On nice days, frequently, the first load would be dry about the time I hung the last. But not always.

Patricia had to be shown how to operate the washing machine so she could do Young Sam's diddies and things twice a week. She seemed to get a good deal of satisfaction from hanging and folding clothes she herself had washed. Truthfully, I was surprised that she had not learned how to do laundry at home. Perhaps the common household chores weren't considered important any longer. Things change—when I was Patricia's age I could manage the entire house for my Mother if the need arose. Anyhow, Patricia did enjoy doing laundry.

Each afternoon I came to prepare supper. While Patricia could dust and do dishes, neither of us had confidence in her ability to put supper on the table. Patricia's work day ended after dinner when the dishes were done and put away. But for several weeks, she stayed over to care for Young Sam's needs during the night. Back then, no one thought anything of a nursemaid working a twelve hour shift five or six days a week. She was quite pleased with the fifteen dollars she received every Saturday. It was as much money as her father was earning. One afternoon she confided that she decided not to mention how much money she was making as it seemed to irritate her Dad. I could see that. Her Dad, my brother, always was a bit of a whiner. Patricia said she opened a savings account and was putting money away for the time when Sam no longer needed her. I thought that was quite smart. She was growing up.

We both had Sundays off. Woody got quite good at diapering and Ted did well with the feeding. They felt it was an equal distribution of chores. I never asked who got up with him during the night. Woody and Ted never mentioned any hardship connected with caring for Sam. I am sure they never had reason to regret keeping him. But, if they did, they never mentioned it.

Young Sam grew. We celebrated his first birthday together. He was walking and beginning to talk. Some words seemed to just roll off his tongue while others were quite difficult for him. He was not a "no" baby—much to my surprise. If Young Sam was asked to do something, he did it. If he was offered a new food, he ate it. If Patricia told him it was nap time, he waddled to the crib kept downstairs and pulled a blanket through the slats. He waited patiently for her to lift him into the crib. I never heard him say no to anything.

At the top of the house there was a beautifully wood paneled room that had been built as a sewing room for Mrs. Olenger. Patricia and I cleaned the room and Ted and Woody bought a bed for Patricia for the nights she would stay over. They said it could be Young Sam's bed when he grew into it. They also bought a second crib. There was already a rocking chair, dresser and a desk in the room. Woody also bought a Philco table radio for Patricia. She was delighted. Her father had a Philco but he seldom listened to things she wanted to hear.

By the time Young Sam was a year old, Woody and Ted felt that they could listen for him during the night every night if he slept in the downstairs' crib. Patricia's workday shrank to twelve hours a day. No more nights. But they still paid her fifteen dollars every Saturday. There were a few nights when they asked her to stay over. Once in a while the brothers would be out of town for business. Woody always made sure Patricia was compensated accordingly. She never minded the extra hours, or money.

Young Sam was a curious boy. He checked out everything at his eyelevel in the house before he was one. And, once he was walking, he began to check out things above his eye level. Many a time Patricia would find him sitting on the dining room table or atop a bookcase. He seemed very careful in his climbing—he never fell and he never broke anything. I thought that was quite unusual but no one else seemed to think on it.

One sunny afternoon, just before Sam turned two, Patricia took him to the backyard to play. She laid a blanket in the sun on the lawn. They watched the gulls and other birds as they enjoyed the pre-summer breezes off the ocean. Then Sam decided he was going to go climbing. Patricia pulled him from a small tree and brought him back to the blanket.

But his little climb had disturbed a hornets' nest; though Patricia swore she never saw one in the tree. A few minutes after they returned to the blanket, a swarm of hornets or perhaps they were bees, literally dive bombed Young Sam. Patricia beat the insects off, picked up the baby and ran for the house. By the time she deposited him in his playpen, he had begun to swell up from the stings. She went to the icebox and chipped ice into a dish towel. She tried to cover the baby's most swelling parts and realized it was a losing battle. His face had swollen so badly his eyes seemed to disappear. He was red and blotchy and a real mess.

Patricia rang to get Central as she was too flustered to remember the ring code for the cannery. Central said she'd send help immediately. Not five minutes later Woody burst through the front door. Patricia was cradling Young Sam and patting his stings with the ice filled towel. Woody blew his top and then realized that wasn't doing any good. And it certainly wasn't something Patricia could have anticipated. Woody got himself under control and asked what happened and she told him through tears . . . insisting she had not seen a hornets' nest in the yard anywhere. Woody said it made no difference if she saw it or not; it obviously was there. He called Ted at the cannery and told him that he and Patricia were going to the doctor in San Luis Obispo. He felt this was beyond the scope of Dr. Johnson's abilities. Would Ted check the yard for a hornets' nest as soon as he got home? He told Ted that Patricia thought it was in the small tree.

Ted thought he should go along to the doctor but Woody said it was more important to rid the yard of pests. He would call from the doctor's office.

The stings were so multiple and serious the doctor put Young Sam in the hospital. So it was a good move on Woody's part to have gone to San Luis Obispo first. Ted arrived about 6pm. He had practically burned the tree to the ground in an effort to destroy the nest which was at the very top of the little tree.

It was a long night for the three of them. The baby went into respiratory arrest before midnight and two hours later into cardiac arrest. Patricia said all of them were crying and praying. Neither brother blamed her but she felt guilty for allowing the attack to happen.

About noon the next day, the doctor came to them in the family room of the pediatric intensive care unit. He had a large smile and the three of them felt the news must be good.

It was. He said that Young Sam had rallied and all his vital signs were normal. He, as a doctor, had never seen such a recovery. But he wanted to keep the baby for at least another day for observation. Why didn't they go home? The doctor suggested they come back the next day. They discussed it between themselves and agreed to do that but not until they had seen Young Sam.

As they walked into the ICU, they could hear Sam cooing in a bassinet. All the nurses were gathered around him making goofy sounds trying to catch his attention. When he saw Woody, he stopped cooing and cried, "Woody, Woody." Then he saw Ted and Patricia and clapped his hands and laughed. The nurses faded away as the three surrounded the bassinet.

Ted spoke to Young Sam as he would an older child. Patricia said he told him we were going to go home and get some sleep. "We've been up all night waiting for you to get better." She said it seemed as though Young Sam undersood every word and grabbed Ted's finger and said, "Night, night, Ted."

Patricia picked him up and told Sam that they all loved him and were happy he was okay now. She said she asked if he hurt anywhere. He told her, "No hurt, Patty, no hurt." She kissed him and put him back into the small bassinet. She told a nurse that he could be rowdy and maybe they should move him into a crib. The nurse said they would watch him closely but they felt he would be warmer and more comfortable in the bassinet.

Woody, Ted and Patricia returned to Cayucos late that afternoon. The boys dropped Patricia at home and promised to keep her informed. Ted called the cannery and told their secretary what had happened and she should not expect them at the wharf before the baby came home.

Early the next morning the doctor called to say he'd just completed his hospital rounds and Young Sam was ready to come home. He couldn't believe the rapid recovery. The stingers were all removed; there was no swelling. There was a bruise or two on Sam's chubby little face. One would never know what a horrendous 24-hours he'd suffered. The brothers said they'd be at the hospital by noon.

As I think back on that episode, I remember Ted was amazed that the charge for the hospitalization was $75. The doctor later sent a bill for $20. Even with my supplemental insurance policy, my co-pay for a single office visit is $20 and just showing up in an emergency room is $50. That ninety-five dollar expense was the total bill for Young Sam—emergency service, two nights in ICU and all the specialized care including the doctor. What a difference in medical costs in seventy years.

There was no insurance back then for people like us. People like Ted and Woody had money. They could afford to pay. So many would not have been able to pay but then, seventy years ago, they would have been treated anyhow. Yes, seventy years bring many changes. Many.

Life went on as usual after Young Sam came home from the hospital. It was a good thing Ted burned out the nest. The first time Patricia and Young

Sam went to the backyard after that, he headed right for the tree. Patricia asked where he was going. He said, "I want to see the buzzers." She told them they had flown away after their tree caught fire.

He toddled around the blackened tree and kept saying something like "Poor buzzers." Patricia said he seemed quite saddened that the hornets were gone. It was half an hour before he settled down enough to pay ball with her.

Young Sam seemed to be different after that—at least, he did to me. Sometimes I would see him sort of tilt his head as though he was listening to something far away. Or he would seem to be staring off into space. I didn't consider that normal behavior for a child not yet two. Perhaps he had always done these things and I hadn't noticed. I don't really know. But somehow there was a difference.

Chapter Five

Sam's second birthday was a gala affair. It was bright and sunny on the fourth of July, 1925. Ted and Woody decided they should host a bar-b-que for everyone who worked in the cannery and on the wharf. The fact that it was also Sam's birthday only made the party happier. All the young people from the cannery lines, the men from the wharf, the secretary, the snooty new male bookkeeper and their families plus Patricia and me filled the huge backyard of the Olenger home.

Most of the workers had seen the house but had never been in the backyard. Woody and two of his workers dug a pit a few days before the 4th and Woody banked a fire which smoldered all day before the party. Three pigs had been dressed out and were slowly roasting on a large spit over the fire. Woody and Ted took turns watching the fire pit and the pigs throughout the night before the fourth. A couple of the single men volunteered to help with the feast—mainly the pig roasting part. By the time I arrived at 9 am, a marvelous aroma drifted through the house.

When Ted and Woody added to the cannery, one of the improvements they made was an employees' room. It had a large refrigerator, a hot plate, wet sink and several long wood tables and benches. All employees brought their dinner from home daily and this room gave them a bright and cozy place to eat.

Before the addition the employees would eat dinner sitting along the edge of the wharf, if the weather was good. If it wasn't, well, then dinner was hurriedly eaten standing under the eaves or along the wall near the cannery line. To accommodate everyone for this fourth of July party, Woody and a couple men took the old Ford stake bed truck to the cannery and loaded the tables and benches. They had been set in place in the yard by the time I got to the house. I covered the tables with sheets—I didn't have tablecloths that large. The party had a much 'fancier' feeling with covered tables. Everyone commented on the table covers. In those days most kitchen tables, where a family ate most meals, was covered with oilcloth. So the table covers indicated this was a very special occasion.

I had cooked for two days to make the several gallons of potato and macaroni salads. I had hard boiled and peeled several dozen eggs to make deviled eggs. And every large jar I could find had been filled the day before with water and tea bags and set in the sun so there would be plenty of tea for the party. The morning of the party I sliced fresh tomatoes and cleaned at least a bushel of fresh vegetables. Ted and Woody were way ahead of their time when it came to picnics. There were several pans of dough rising to be re-kneaded one more time before being baked into sandwich rolls. Woody had a large pot of spicy sauce simmering on the stove to be slathered on the pork as it was served.

The stove was a beautiful white porcelain model with a large cooking area of four burners. The oven box sat to the right of the cooking area. No leaning over needed to use it. Old Mr. Olenger had ordered the stove especially for Mrs. Olenger back in 1910 from some manufacturer on the East Coast. The oven was oversized and I knew I would have to fill it only three or four times to bake all the sandwich rolls.

By noon the backyard was filled with chattering, happy people. There were several different age groups. There were the old timers who had been at the cannery when it was only one line and a minor part of the wharf business. Many had graduated high school around the time I had. Most of the cannery girls were young—under twenty. The wharf workers were in their 20s or early 30s though there were a couple of old timers in their 40s and 50s.

The last couple to arrive was Glenn and Connie Jackson. Glenn said they had hesitated to come because Tommy, their baby, wasn't very strong. Tommy was not quite eight months old. He couldn't tolerate mother's milk when he was born and cow's milk wasn't any better. Dr. Johnson suggested goat's milk and that seemed to be okay. But Tommy hadn't grown like an average child. In fact, he was swaddled in a basket hung over Glenn's arm looking almost like a newborn.

The back steps of the Olenger house are wide and sheltered and Glenn deposited the basket on the bottom step before joining his friends and co-workers. Connie frequently came to check on the baby. He seemed to sleep an awful lot. Well, that was my opinion.

About 12:30 or so, Ted and Woody decided the feast should begin. Everyone lined up with his plate in hand to pass the bar-b-que pit. Ted sliced and served and Woody slathered on the sauce. Then everyone helped himself to the food set out on one table before finding a place to sit and eat. The eating went on for quite a while. Ted and Woody both ate standing up that day, as I recall, to be sure everyone was accommodated. I brought my plate back to the porch steps and sat there to eat. I could keep an eye on the food and replenish as needed and still enjoy my dinner.

Young Sam must have thought he was in the grandest place on earth. He had a piece of meat in one fist and a celery stick in the other. He went visiting all the people. Some offered him a bite of something and he'd open his mouth wide and accept it. He never let go of the food he had in his hands. After chewing and swallowing he'd say, "Thank you." before checking out the next group. Young Sam loved people. I am sure he had never seen so many in one place before and he was thoroughly enjoying himself. I asked Patricia to keep an eye on him but to let him roam. Periodically she'd grab him and wash his hands and face. He was having the time of his life.

As dinner seemed to be breaking up, some games started, Sam came to the porch where I was sitting and sat along side me for quite awhile. He was very curious about the baby in the basket on the bottom step. I told him the baby wasn't feeling too well but he could touch him if he wanted to. Sam loved to touch people. He offered his hands to me to be washed.

Sam sat on the step next to the basket for some time. He had a one-way conversation with Tommy. At least, at first it was one way. Coming back into the house with an empty bowl, I heard Sam talk to Tommy and Tommy replied. It was all gurgle and coo but was definitely a reply. I watched Sam as he held Tommy's hand while he talked to him.

Please understand that Sam's language skills were not all that great even though he was two. He always made himself understood even if the words were sometimes nothing more than gibberish. So listening to a two-year old speak to an eight-month old was not informative, only amusing.

Sam would wander away from the basket from time to time to see what was going on in the backyard. But he returned frequently, perhaps to update Tommy on what was happening. Connie came twice and took Tommy inside to change his diaper. She remarked how alert he appeared, much more than usual. I told her Sam had been talking to him and perhaps that was the reason. She just smiled and said, "Perhaps that's it." I only meant that perhaps having someone younger talk to him encouraged Tommy. I don't know what she thought I meant.

There was a pause in the fun and games around 4 and I brought out dessert—a large birthday cake.

I had also baked a sheet cake to be sure everyone had cake. Sam was delighted. He stood on a bench and watched the two candles as they burned down. When they were almost to the cake, he leaned over and blew them out. He clapped his hands and yelled, "Happy birthday, Sam." Everyone laughed and lined up for cake. Nearly everyone echoed him as they took a piece. "Happy birthday, Sam." He was so excited.

The summer sky is lit for hours—even after sundown. About seven, people began drifting away, most having eaten a second time. Woody and his crew stripped the tables and took them and the benches back to the cannery. I could see that I would have a lot of laundry to do Monday. I wondered if perhaps I should come tomorrow and do just the sheets from today.

Sam seemed genuinely sorry to see everyone leave. When Glenn picked up the basket, Sam ran to him and peered over the rim and gibberished something to Tommy. Tommy responded in kind. Sam followed Glenn to the front gate and stood there waving and shouting goodbyes. Finally he came back to the yard to watch us restore it to pre-party status. The young men who helped dig the pit now helped fill it in. There was very little meat left over. Woody put it on a platter and I took it inside. I had been trying to keep up all afternoon with the dishes so there wouldn't be too many to do at once. But, even so, there were quite a few things at the end of the day that needed to be washed. Woody came in and offered to dry as I washed. I thanked him but said it was under control. He asked, "Do you think my Dad would have approved of this shindig, Mrs. Willoughby?"

I dried my hands on my apron. "Woody, I think he would have been delighted."

He kissed me on the cheek and went back to doing whatever he'd been doing before he came in. He and Ted came in 20 minutes later. Ted asked, "Is that coffee I smell?"

I got down three mugs. "I thought maybe it would be welcomed about now."

We toasted each other with our coffee mugs. Ted said, "It was a damned good party, wasn't it?" Woody and I nodded. It certainly was.

Patricia gave Sam a bath and he came into the kitchen all clean and rosy to say goodnight to Ted, Woody and me. He climbed on Ted's knee and gave him a big kiss and said, "I liked the party, Ted." Then he climbed down and went to Woody. Woody lifted him up and said, "I'm glad you liked the party, Sam. Happy birthday."

"I'm this many." Sam held up two chubby fingers. We all laughed.

It had been a very fine bar-b-que and the first of many to come. Old Mr. Olenger had been good to his employees but had never hosted a company party—like this or any other. The workers talked about this particular party for years to come. It had been a very special time.

At the time, I didn't know how special. Two months, or so, after the bar-b-que, I met Connie Jackson in the community store. She had she had been planning to come up and see me some afternoon but hadn't gotten to it. She was glad we had met when we did. She wanted to tell me that since the party, Tommy seemed to thrive. He began to grow; the growth that hadn't happened in his first eight months suddenly seemed to happen. He was far too big now for the basket. He had nearly caught up to where he should be at ten months. Tommy was crawling everywhere and pulling himself up on things. Connie thought he would be walking by the time he was a year old.

At the time, I thought nothing of it. The child just finally started to develop. Doesn't delayed development happen sometimes? He didn't start out well with his milk allergy and all. But I told her how glad I was and asked about the allergy. It had disappeared. She had run out of goat's milk two weeks ago but Tommy wanted milk. She gave him an ounce of cow's milk. There was no adverse reaction. He drinks cow's milk all the time now. I suggested that perhaps that was part of the natural growth—people outgrow allergies all the time. Maybe his digestive system hadn't completely developed before. She said that was what the doctor believed.

Ah, babies. Who really knows everything about them?

Chapter Six

The day after the party there was a red American Flyer wagon on the front porch. It was Young Sam's only birthday gift. Ted and Woody thought it would be better to not give it to him at the party as no one had been told it was a birthday party. Instead, it was a company 4th of July party. The birthday cake was the only hint that it was more than that.

Patricia was delighted with the wagon as much as Sam was. She had wanted to take Sam to the beach and into town and just 'do things'. But Sam was too heavy to carry and too little to walk as far as Patricia might want to go. After the party, most afternoons as I arrived at the house to make supper, Patricia and Sam would be coming home too, from their day out. Sometimes Patricia's boyfriend would walk them home. He worked at the community store and got off work at 3 during the week.

Patricia put a blanket in the wagon and set Sam on it. Most days she would pack a lunch and a thermos of water so they could leave early and come home late. Sam was browning up like a little nut ripening in the sun. His blond hair was now sun bleached. I must admit, he was a very handsome two-year old.

One Saturday I arrived at the house and Patricia and Sam were not there. It was nearly suppertime before they showed up. Both were soaking wet and looking quite bedraggled. I asked what in the world happened and Patricia said she'd tell me as she gave Sam a bath. Usually Woody gave him a bath after supper but she insisted. He needed a bath—now. Sam was full of sand and there were bottom rocks in his short little pants. I demanded that she tell me what had happened as it was obvious something had.

"Well," she began a bit hesitantly. "There was some fool tourist standing on the north pier fishing. I'm not sure what he was fishing for though as he never caught anything that we saw. Sam and I were sitting in the shade of the pier. All of a sudden there was a big splash and a loud yell. I don't know if he fell or jumped but all of a sudden he was directly in front of us in the water. I think he hit his head on one of the pilings on his way down though. He went under. He looked unconscious to me."

She went on to say that she started yelling for help but no one came. She ran to the water's edge and waded in after the man. By this time he was bobbing up and down with the motion of the waves. She grabbed hold of his arms and pulled him onto the sand. He wasn't breathing. Patricia had worked as a lifeguard one summer down in Morro Bay and knew what to do. She rolled him over and started pumping water out of him. She thought he was dead, for sure. After about ten minutes, she gave up trying to get him to breathe. She told Sam to stay where he was and she ran up to the street looking for help.

When she got back with Danny Johansson in tow, Sam was sitting on the man's chest—talking to him. The man was alive after all. He was dazed and couldn't remember what had happened. He insisted he didn't remember anything until Sam started babbling to him. He said it was like coming out of a long hard sleep. Though Sam talked to him all the time Patricia was gone, he said he understood very little of what Sam said but somehow had the impression that Sam had been responsible for him coming back to life.

Patricia couldn't explain how Sam had gotten so wet. She had pulled the man way above the water line. Sam kept telling her the fishies told him to wake up the man. So, he did. Danny took charge of the tourist. He made sure the tourist knew Patricia had been the one who saved him—who went into the water and pulled him out. But Patricia insisted, and does to this very day, that when she left the beach for help, the man was dead.

When Woody and Ted came in for supper they congratulated Patricia for saving the man's life. It was all over town that Patricia and Sam had been responsible for pulling a tourist out of the ocean. The doctor later said it was possible when Sam sat on the man's chest and rocked to and fro, he created a rhythm that restarted the man's heart.

Patricia didn't protest too much while the boys were shaking her hand but she told me later that Sam was there—he saved the guy, not her. She knew for sure he was dead when she left the beach.

Sam was quite tired that evening; Patricia said he nearly fell asleep in his potatoes. We guessed all the excitement wore him out. But he also slept in the next morning. He was asleep when Patricia arrived so she fed him breakfast long after Ted and Woody had gone.

A week later Patricia showed me a cashier's check for a hundred dollars that the tourist's family had sent to her as a token of their gratitude. She wanted to give it to Sam but I told her Sam was well cared for—she should keep it.

A hundred dollars was a lot of money in 1925.

Chapter Seven

The summer seemed to zip by after that. And fall, then winter, came to Cayucos. There hadn't been a Christmas tree in the house since Mrs. Olenger passed. But the boys decided there should be one this year. Sam was old enough to get excited about it, they figured. And he was.

They didn't hang stockings that year but Sam got a large metal dump truck. He pushed it all around the house. Patricia said she could hardly wait until summer so he could go to the beach and play in the sand with it.

1926 had started out blustery, wet and miserable. The ocean was so rough that many ships docked at the TWO Wharf and stayed for several days. The cannery was closed. No one could fish for anything in weather like that. The waves were higher than I had seen them in years. Sam would sit on the front porch steps all bundled up and watch the ocean.

Finally, one afternoon in March, the sun came out and the temperatures rose to above 60. Patricia pulled the red wagon which now carried both Sam and his truck down the front walk. They were headed for the beach. The sun was shining brightly, the wind had calmed to gentle off-shore breezes. It hadn't rained for two days. They spent a couple hours on the water's edge. I met them as I was going to the house to make supper.

Patricia said they had watched a sea gull for a while. He appeared drunk as he staggered in circles on the beach. Though she warned Sam to leave the bird alone, he insisted on checking it out. The gull stopped its circling and seemed to watch Sam. Without any warning, Sam picked up the large bird. Patricia said she yelled at him to drop the bird. It was so large she was afraid the gull would hurt him—peck him if nothing else. She went running to where Sam stood holding it.

Sam told her the bird wouldn't hurt him. The bird wasn't feeling too good. He sat down with the gull in his lap and crooned to it for more than five minutes. Then he sat he bird down on the beach. Sam took Patricia by the hand and said, "He's okay now. Let's go home." Patricia said she more than willing to leave. She's afraid of seagulls, especially the larger ones, as she had been badly pecked when she was six or seven. Otherwise, she said she would have taken the bird away from Sam. He didn't seem to have any problems with it. She hurriedly loaded everything, Sam and his truck, back into the wagon before he could change his mind. By the time they reached the walk at the top of the beach, the seagull was walking just fine. She said she stopped at the top of the bluff and watched him take off over the water. His take off was smooth and even. His flight was regular.

Patricia said, "Aunt Agnes, it's unnatural the way Sam talks to animals and birds. And he insists they talk back. It kind of scares me."

I nodded. I knew just how she felt. But talking to the animals wasn't the only thing that bothered me about Sam.

And, that's how it began. I am sure that every single event had a logical explanation. But I also know that Sam had some sort of 'power'. For the next two years, until he was four, I witnessed, or heard from Patricia, more than a dozen episodes where Sam seemingly healed someone or something; restored them to whole or otherwise made them feel better. Patricia and I agreed that we should keep our mouths shut. First of all, no one would believe us. Secondly, if they did, then people would be watching Sam 24/7 for his next 'miracle'. He was just a little boy but somehow he was "different".

Just before Sam's fourth birthday my sister-in-law, Patricia's mother, became quite ill. There didn't seem to be a name for her malady or a treatment locally. She couldn't afford to travel to San Francisco to see a specialist. She slowly withered away. Finally, one Monday morning while I was doing the laundry at the Olenger house, Patricia asked me if I truly believed Sam had some sort of magic. I told her I truly did. She said she did too and wanted my permission to take Sam to visit her mother.

As it was usual for Patricia and Sam to go all over town together, I told her that if she wanted to visit her one weekday morning—rather than on Sunday—it would be logical that Sam would go with her. She understood that I meant she should visit her mother mid-week. Sam would go with her then as he was her charge during the week. She never required permission from Ted or Woody to go anywhere and there would be no reason for that to change if she wanted to visit her mother. Frankly, I would have thought she had visited her mother many times since being Sam's nanny. But evidently not.

Patricia and Sam went to visit Patricia's mother. Sam sat on a throw rug close to the divan when she was resting. He just sat there and watched her. Patricia and her mother chatted for about an hour. Patricia said she told her mother she didn't want to tire her so they would come back to visit perhaps on Thursday. She had not ever mentioned Sam's 'powers' to her mother and did not do so now.

Sam was his usual lively self that evening at dinner.

On Thursday, they returned and Sam sat on the throw rug watching Patricia's mother until Patricia got up to leave. Then he went to her mother, patted her hand and said, "I'm sorry you don't feel good, Nannie."

No one had told Sam Patricia's mother's name or nickname and Patricia couldn't recall every mentioning it in his hearing. Only close family called Nancy Nannie.

Sam was his usual lively self that evening at dinner.

On Saturday that week they returned. Nancy was sitting on the divan as if waiting for them. Sam went directly to her and climbed up and sat next to her. He put his arms around her and hugged her as tightly as a four-year old can. Then he sat down on the throw rug and watched her as she and Patricia visited.

Sam asked to go to bed early that night.

On Monday Patricia told me her mother was feeling much better. She had visited with her again on Sunday. Her mother was sitting at the kitchen table having a cup of tea that she had made herself. She had not done anything so strenuous for weeks.

Tuesday Patricia and Sam went visiting Nancy again. She was delighted her daughter would walk all the way across the town to see her—especially with Sam in tow. Patricia said she told her mother that she was just worried about her health. Nancy said she was feeling so much better. And she certainly appreciated the visits.

On that Tuesday Nancy was on her front porch sitting in the glider swing when Patricia and Sam arrived. Without invitation, Sam climbed up on the swing next to her and snuggled against her. Nancy was surprised but said perhaps he felt he knew her well enough now for a hug. He stayed next to her while Patricia went into the house and got them both a glass of lemonade. He sat on the top porch step and drank his lemonade and hummed a little tuneless tune. When they were ready to leave, he hugged Nancy and waved goodbye. Patricia pulled the wagon down the front walk. When she got to the street she turned and called to her mother that they might not be back for a week or so as she had been neglecting a few chores around the house and wanted to catch up before Woody or Ted noticed.

I was preparing supper when they came home that afternoon.

"Aunt Agnes, I believe we are right about Sam. Mother is almost as well as she's ever been. She says she feels better than she has in years."

By the time supper was ready, Sam was sound asleep on the sofa in the living room. Both Woody and Ted asked Patricia how she had managed that. Sam was always such a live wire. He actually was quiet all during supper though he ate more than usual.

We swore each other to secrecy and hoped that nothing big would occur that would call attention to Sam's apparent healing abilities.

The summer came and went and winter was on us again. The wind was unusually cruel that winter. I can't remember it ever being so cold before in Cayucos. Patricia and I both arrived at the Olenger house bundled up nearly every day in December and January. It was almost too cold to be out.

As I recall, that winter was the only time in my life that I wished I had a car.

The following summer, when Sam was five, something did happen that caused a lot of people to first doubt themselves and then speculate about Sam.

The summer had been unusually cool through the middle of July. The company picnic had become an annual thing now and everyone looked forward to it, even though the temperature was only mid-70s. It had become a potluck the previous year I think except for the meat and sandwich rolls. A few of the cannery girls thought it would be more fair and fun at the same time. This eased my workload a lot and the workers all felt they were a greater part of the picnic . . . which they were. The picnic was still in the Olenger back yard but there was a general feeling of ownership that one day every year. The single guys were usually the ones who helped dig the pit and watch the spit.

Tommy Jackson was a picture of health. No one could ever imagine he was the weak little baby swaddled in a basket at the first picnic a few years earlier. He and Sam played well together whenever they saw each other. They had a grand time at the company picnic. They visited table by table, eating their way across the yard. I was surprised that neither of them was sick the night of the picnic. They ate a lot—of everything.

Well, as I was saying, summer had been a bit cool which disappointed the tourists who liked to fish off the Cayucos public pier and lay around on the little beach in the cove. The weather didn't keep them from coming though. They just didn't do as much laying around on the beach. Not only was there a lack of sun but there was a cold breeze nearly every day. Then, like now only not so blatant, some of the summer visitors just didn' t know how to recognize property lines. More than once I'd arrive at the Olenger house and have to shoo a party off the front lawn. And there was a fence! The beach was a hundred yards or so away but the lush green lawn and the shelter of the large shade trees beckoned to them.

One afternoon I arrived at the house to find Patricia and Sam, in his wagon, at the front gate arguing with a party of three young men. Patricia was on the outside of the fence and they were on the inside. I am sure they knew she lived there but were having sport with her and wouldn't let her through the gate.

When I arrived, by shank's mare of course, they looked a bit amused until I told them to get off the property or else. One rather husky boy swaggered to the gate and said, "Or else what?"

I told him I would call the local law on him. Well, he just laughed at that. He was pretty sure there was no local law. He was not a local and I suppose, because Cayucos was so small, he figured there wouldn't be any local law. In those days, we didn't all carry cell phones as we do now. I told Patricia to go down to the cannery office and get Ted. She left Sam sitting in his wagon. I opened the gate, having to push rather forcefully and pulled Sam and the wagon inside the fence. Surprisingly, the trio backed up enough to allow me entrance. I think I took them unawares. They hadn't expected me to try and enter as long as they were there, a menacing force inside the gate.

I took Sam out of the wagon and whispered in his ear to go into the house and ring Central for help. He nodded and ran as fast as he could. One of the boys made a move as if to stop him but Sam slipped right past him. The boy shrugged. He probably thought we didn't have telephones either in such a small town.

Ted and Patricia arrived right after Sam entered the house. The three were intimidated somewhat now. There was a man on the premises. Ted was tall for the times and well built. He would have intimidated me, I believe. Ted asked who they were and what they were trying to prove. They swaggered a bit and one started to bluster out a response. The other two turned on him and told him to shut his mouth.

Ted stood firm. "Who are you and what do you want at my house?"

I believe they were unaware he owned the house before this moment. None of them had an answer. He asked them to leave. Very politely he asked. They stood silent as if daring him to back up his request with force. But that wasn't Ted's way.

They had strewn trash and a blanket across the yard. He told them to pick up their trash as they left. It was a direct order. "Pick up your trash on your way out." One did lean down and begin to gather bottles and papers. The bully who had confronted Patricia and me shoved him backwards and told him to leave the crap where it was. He picked up a bottle and, holding it by the neck, whacked it on the fence. The bottle broke into a jagged weapon. I hadn't realized before then that he was drunk—much more so than the other two—which probably accounted for his bravado. I am sure all three had been drinking but this one was definitely inebriated.

"Come on, Old Man. Make me leave." His companions seemed to be trying to divorce themselves from him and were sidling around toward the gate.

About that time I could see a car coming. The local sheriff. Sam's call to Central had brought help and just in the nick of time, I thought. The Sheriff stopped at the end of the walk and decided he'd handcuff the two trying to run from the yard. He threw them both in the back seat of his patrol car.

The third was still waving his broken bottle. The Sheriff came through the gate and motioned to Ted that he'd go around behind the drunk and between the two of them, they could subdue him. The Sheriff grabbed for the arm holding the bottle and Ted tackled the boy's legs. He went down but the bottle slashed Ted's upper arm and shoulder. He was bleeding badly. The Sheriff handcuffed the third boy and threw him into the car. The Sheriff shouted he'd send medical help immediately.

I couldn't believe the Sheriff was leaving when Ted was obviously badly injured. Patricia and I helped Ted into the house and sat him on a chair in the kitchen. I sent Patricia to get some of Sam's old diapers from the hall cupboard. The cut was deep. I could see muscle. We made the diapers into compresses to staunch the flow of blood. Sam came into the kitchen, very white faced.

"Ted, are you okay?" Sam was a bit taller than the average five-year old and came almost to Ted's shoulder when he was sitting. It appeared that Ted was making an attempt to reply but couldn't quite get words out. He nodded. Even so, it was obvious, he was not okay.

I said to Sam, "Here, you hold this compress against Ted as tight as you can while I make an ice pack."

Patricia looked at me and mouthed, "Are you sure we want to do this?"

"We don't have a choice. Ted is damn near bleeding to death." And he was. There was a lot of blood. Patricia went for more diapers. Sam solemnly held first one compress and then another and crooned to Ted the whole while. Ted was getting pasty looking. I was scared. I hoped the medical help the Sheriff promised would be soon in coming. I had heard of people bleeding out but never thought I'd see it happen.

I took the second compress from Sam to put on another, filled with ice. Sam looked at the deep gash and said to Ted, "You have a really bad cut, Ted." I laid the new compress on and Sam held it tightly. I was sure Ted would pass out any second. He was looking bad. I asked Patricia to help me and we stretched Ted out on the kitchen floor. I don't know how I thought that would help. Sam insisted on holding Ted's head on his lap. Patricia took over the compress. Sam kept asking, "Are you okay, Ted?" Ted mumbled an answer though I wasn't sure what it was.

I asked Patricia to ring Central and see if she could locate Doctor Johnson. Perhaps the Sheriff hadn't made contact. Central said that the Sheriff had come in and asked her to locate the doctor and send him to the house. I heard Patricia say, "Central, Ted is dying. Please, send help."

It was nearly fifteen minutes more before Doctor Johnson came to the front door. Patricia yelled at him to come in; that we were all in the kitchen.

By this time we had a half dozen blood soaked diaper compresses in a pan and Ted was almost comatose. The doctor paled as he looked at the wound. "We need to get Ted to the hospital and get some blood into him. He's damn near bled out but the wound looks clean. Why the hell didn't the Sheriff bring him in instead of those hooligans? I'm sorry Agnes, but it will be a miracle if he makes it. He's lost a lot of blood."

Patricia rang the Cannery and Woody was there in seconds. The two men put Ted into the back seat of Doc's car. Woody rode crouched on the floor between the front and back seats. Patricia was in tears and I was at the point I thought I couldn't hold my tears back much longer.

Sam helped as we cleaned up the kitchen and then cleared the trash from the yard. It was a couple of hours before we heard from Woody. Ted would be okay. Perhaps he hadn't lost as much blood as the Doc figured. When he was brought into the emergency room his blood pressure didn't even register. He was unconscious. The hospital had only one pint of Ted's blood type on hand. But by the time the transfusion was complete, Ted's blood pressure was almost normal. The Doc was amazed. Woody asked where Sam had been during the crisis. I told him he held an ice pack to Ted's shoulder almost the entire time. Woody said something like, "I kind of figured something like that."

That surprised me. Perhaps Patricia and I weren't the only ones who had seen something different about Sam.

I had cleaned the kitchen. I know how much blood he had lost. It was a hell of a lot. Patricia and I hugged Sam closely. "Ted is going to be okay, Sam. Thank you for helping."

And Sam said, "You're welcome. I knew he'd be okay."

The doctor stopped by later that evening. Patricia and I hadn't gone home yet—we were waiting for Woody. The doctor wanted to know what had happened before he got there. He had seen the compresses and the floor and both Patricia and me. He was quite sure Ted had lost several pints of blood. I went through what we'd done; step-by-step. Sam was the only unknown ingredient. Doctor Johnson asked how Sam had taken the injury.

I told him he had held the compresses to the wound and talked to Ted the entire time. He'd taken it as though it was something that could happen any day. He didn't seem frightened? No, not at all. The doctor stroked his chin and looked thoughtful. "Well, I'm glad he wasn't scared. I know his being there was comforting to Ted."

Patricia and I wondered what else the Doctor had in mind. What else had he seen or heard or noticed? The tourist on the beach? He wasn't around for the seagull. What? But there was no doubt in my mind that evening that the good doctor also thought there was something unusual about Sam.

The town was appalled at what had happened and began a program to patrol the beaches and beach front properties more often. The three boys were drunk and deemed unaccountable. However, Ted did press charges against the one who had slashed him. The stabbing was accidental but Ted felt that there was no other way to make the boy accountable as the law seemed to think drunkenness was an excuse to not prosecute. The boy turned out to be 20 years old. The two with him were teenagers. The court agreed with Ted and the 20-year old spent 30-days in jail. Restitution was ordered as well. The boy wrote Ted a note apologizing for his behavior and the injury he did to Ted and his property. Ted said he'd keep it as reminder that sometimes it pays to prosecute—maybe the kid learned a lesson.

Personally, I doubted it.

Ted was on light duty for some time but returned, good as new before the month was over. Someone had started a rumor that Sam was a miracle worker of some sort. We tried to play it down. Then Connie Jackson remembered how sick Tommy had been until Sam played with him. And, of course, my sister-in-law—she never could keep her mouth shut. And the tourist on the beach—well, he was just another part of a really good story. We tried to keep it just that—a good story. We reasoned Sam just happens to be in the right places to make it appear he may have had something to do with whatever was going on. We tried to convince other people that's how it was. Sam's presence was always just a coincidence.

But Patricia and I knew different by this time. There was definitely something special about Sam. For the rest of the summer we tried to keep Sam away from people. Of course, he rebelled about that. Sam was a people person even at age five. Thinking back on it, he'd been a people person his entire life. Sam reveled in people.

The summer was beautiful the next year. The ocean was frequently so calm it looked like a very large mirror. Cayucos is a very small town and depends on tourists quite a bit. Most of the men worked out of town as there wasn't a lot of commerce in Cayucos. The town is not very wide and the furthest point from the ocean is less than a mile. Even back in the 20s there were a couple of small motels and summer only type restaurants. The population has never been great—not then and not now. But many of those summer only restaurants are now open year round and there are a few more motels. I guess in these sixty some years very little has actually changed in Cayucos. The cannery and commercial wharf are gone. There is a long public pier that draws visitors year round. But the town itself is more or less what it was in the 1920s and 1930s.

But back to the story . . . sometimes I get carried away with memories of this small town.

In late August I was purchasing some yardage at the local emporium. Mr. Harrad, the proprietor, was measuring and cutting what I wanted. There was no one near the cutting board but the two of us. He asked me about Sam and his healing abilities. Did I really believe in them? I told him I had seen some things but they could all be explained away. He pressed me "Do you believe?"

I asked why he was inquiring. It seemed odd to me that a middle-aged man in obvious good health would be curious about such a thing. He confided that his wife was ailing badly and had been for most of the summer. He was sure she would die from blood loss or anemia before long if something didn't help her. The doctor was at a loss.

He practically begged me to visit his wife and take Sam with me. I told him that would be highly unethical of me. It would create speculation and I didn't want to expose Sam to that sort of publicity. Mrs. Harrad and I know one another but we were not 'visiting' friends. He asked if I would consider delivering a package to his home for him?

Just then Patricia and Sam came to the cutting table. They had been out on the town and saw me come into the store. Patricia sensed something unusual was happening and she looked at me questioningly. I was torn between possibly helping another human being and exploiting Sam. I told her that Mr. Harrad had promised to take a roast home to his wife the night before and forgotten. She was counting on it for supper tonight. He was looking for a messenger.

As Mr. Harrad and a young clerk worked the store alone, it was a feasible situation. I told her that I had told him I wouldn't be able to do it. Patricia caught on right away and said she and Sam could take the package.

Mr. Harrad said that by the time we'd finished shopping, he'd have the package ready. He added, "Thank you so much. I might not get supper otherwise." He laughed at his own small joke and patted Sam on the head.

True to his word, there was a small wrapped package tied in string at the register when we had finished shopping. Patricia put Sam into his wagon and handed him the package. We went out together. Patricia asked me quite directly, "Aunt Agnes, what's the real story here?"

I told her what Mr. Harrad had told me about his wife. He had heard rumors about Sam and was desperate enough to ask for this favor. And I told him that we could not say that Sam could help that everything was coincidental and the rumors were just that. And it would appear odd if I were to take Sam—it would emphasize his presence there.

"If you hadn't come in just then, his request would have been denied. It seemed providential to me that you would come into the store when you did. Like perhaps this was something we should do."

I went directly home as I didn't have to be at the Olenger house until mid-afternoon. I was deeply upset with myself that I was allowing Sam to be exploited in this manner. If there's a God in heaven he would surely smite me dead at any moment. It was a terrible conflict—everyone deserves the chance to live and thrive and if the medical world can't help, what do you do? But it was exposing Sam to what kind of danger? I knew that some of these "healings" had taken much out of Sam. Was I shortening his life by allowing him to do a good deed? It was definitely exploitation. I have seldom felt so miserable as I did that afternoon.

When I arrived at the Olenger house later, Patricia said, "Aunt Agnes, that poor woman looks like walking death. She came to the door and, at first, wasn't going to let us in. I told her that Mr. Harrad had asked us to deliver a package to her on our way home. She still hesitated and then it seems like she saw the package in Sam's hands and realized we were friendly. She invited us in and Sam handed her the package. She patted his head and said thank you. Sam took hold of her hand with both of his. She stood stock still for a minute and got a really odd look on her face. Sam started telling her how sorry he was that she wasn't feeling too good but he knew she'd feel better soon. Aunt Agnes, I could see something change in her as I watched; something in her face. I don't know what it was. It was spooky."

While Patricia was telling me this Sam was sitting on a kitchen stool. He was within hearing range but I believe he didn't hear a word. He had a far off look in his eyes and sat there, stock still.

Patricia said that Mrs. Harrad thanked them again for delivering the roast. There really was a roast in the package. Mrs Harrad leaned down and hugged Sam. He hugged her and kissed her cheek.

"Kissed her check? That's not very Sam like. He likes hugs but kisses?"

"I know, Aunt Agnes, it was creepy. And he's been in a really strange mood ever since."

I looked at Sam. Odd mood was right. He was staring at nothing; just sitting on the stool. But, was it an odd mood or was he exhausted? I began to worry again about what I had allowed to happen and breathed a small prayer that Sam would be all right.

Patricia wanted to leave before Ted and Woody got home. I told her to go ahead. She'd been seeing a young man and I was sure it was serious. She was twenty and more than ready to marry. She mentioned to Ted she was thinking of getting married but would wait until Sam started school the next fall.

Sam sat on that stool for the next hour and some while I was preparing supper. Staring at nothing and not moving. Finally, about ten minutes before Woody and Ted were due home, he jumped off the stool and went outside and ran around the house twice. Then he went and stood on the front gate waiting for the two men. As soon as he saw them, he swung open the gate and went running to meet them—just as he did every other day.

Woody grabbed Sam and tossed him in the air. Ted said, "Watch it, Woody. The boy is getting heavy. You don't want to drop him."

But Sam wasn't afraid. He didn't squeal or cry out. He knew Woody would never drop him on purpose.

The three of them came up the front steps together. Ted asked how my afternoon had been. I told him just fine. He sniffed. "What is that lovely aroma, Mrs. Willoughby? It smells good enough to eat." I replied that I certainly would hope so. He half smiled as though he wasn't sure if I was joking or hadn't realized he was. I guess I could be a little stern in those days.

They washed up at the sink on the back porch; Sam included. After Woody dried Sam's hands and hung the towel, they came in for supper. Once the meal was on the table, I said my goodnights. Sam waved goodbye with a biscuit in each hand. The two men said they'd see me tomorrow and I left.

Sam was all wound up now and I could hear him chattering away as I left myself out. I was hoping that he wouldn't say anything about the visit to Mrs. Harrad. I was quite sure neither of them would approve of my allowing what had happened to happen. I was definitely exploiting Sam. I felt pretty bad as I walked home. I shouldn't have allowed it; I knew it. But even now, thinking back, I believe I would do it again. Mrs. Harrad lived a very long and productive life.

When I got to the house the next afternoon Patricia told me that Sam was still asleep when she got there just before seven. Woody had teased her about wearing Sam out the day before and she said that she had replied something to the effect that they had walked a lot. Patricia said Sam slept until 8 but had been himself once he was up and had eaten breakfast.

I told her that I believed we should not have allowed Sam to go to Mrs. Harrad's. Whatever happened between them sucked a lot of vitality out of Sam. And it was so soon after the Ted episode I was afraid whatever energy young boys store had been depleted. Patricia agreed we should avoid this type of thing from now on. She said she had felt pretty bad about it too.

Sam slept in every morning for the rest of that week. By mid-September he was his usual live wire, up at 6, self. It appeared that Ted and Woody never realized the difference in the boy. Ted did mention it was strange for Sam to be sleeping so late but Woody felt that growing boys sometimes need more sleep. They have always pooh-poohed his "abilities" anyhow—even after Ted's miracle recovery.

Autumn came to Cayucos swiftly. The trees seemed to change color overnight. Winter seemed imminent—already in October. The wind never let up the entire month. It was cold, damp and a perpetual mist hung over the town. Fog moved in before sunset and seldom dissipated before noon. By the end of November we were all tired of winter and it hadn't even begun yet.

Chapter Eight

In January Patricia's family moved to Morro Bay and Patricia moved in with me. My little house had two bedrooms and it was convenient for us both.

Then, in early March, my sister-in-law, Patricia's mother fell and broke both her wrists. It was an odd fall and, according to the doctor, an even odder set of breaks. Patricia asked Woody and Ted if she could take two weeks off to go to Morro Bay to help her mother. Of course, they said yes. But that put them in a bit of a ruffle as Young Sam wasn't in school yet. It was apparent (to me) they thought it was too much of an imposition to ask me to come at 7. I didn't want to see Sam at the cannery all day and it would be impractical for either of the Olengers to stay at home until I arrived in the afternoon. So I volunteered.

The second week of March started bright and sunny. It looked like the weather would hold a few days so I decided it would be a good time to start Spring cleaning at the Olengers. I would begin with the curtains. The Olengers have a small step stool and a tall ladder; neither really suitable to take down and hang up curtains. So, on Monday, I set out for the Olenger house with my three-step ladder over my shoulder.

I had not gone a block before I saw Woody Olenger approaching. "Well, good morning, Woody! What are you doing in my neck of the woods this early in the morning?"

"I came to carry your ladder for you. Sam said you'd be bringing it today to take down the curtains."

At that, I nearly dropped the ladder. I had not mentioned Spring cleaning to anyone, let alone Sam. And I certainly hadn't told him I would be bringing my ladder with me Monday. Not really knowing how to react, I just handed the ladder to Woody and said, "Thank you."

We chit-chatted as we walked the remaining few blocks. He wondered if he needed to enroll Sam for school before the end of this school term. He commented on how tall Sam was and said he felt he'd be four feet tall by his sixth birthday. I told him it was customary to enroll before the first day of school but not necessarily before the last day of school.

I didn't mention that I hadn't told Sam about the step ladder. I was anxious for Patricia to return. How long has this type of foreseeing been going on? Or was this a first? I wasn't frightened but very concerned. What else is there I don't know about this child?

After Ted and Woody had left for work I asked Sam, "How did you know I was going to bring my ladder today?"

"I just knew. You said I really need to get those curtains washed. I'll have to bring my step-ladder with me tomorrow. So I told Uncle Woody this morning."

"You knew this yesterday? I wasn't here yesterday. It was Sunday."

"I know. But you told me anyway."

I thanked him and asked if he had told Woody that I hadn't actually said anything.

"Oh, no, then he wouldn't have gone to help you. But Mrs. Willoughby, you did tell me."

I wanted to ask him if he dreamed our conversation. But he seemed so adamant that I had told him. And I did remember actually saying those very words to myself Sunday afternoon. Somehow this didn't seem like a first-time incident. Perhaps other things had come up and Sam said he dreamed it so nothing was done. I was truly anxious then for Patricia to return—and she'd been gone only a week.

On Good Friday, I arrived at Olenger's just after 3pm. The cannery and wharf closed at 11 that morning so everyone could go to church. Back in those days, everyone went to a tannebrae service on Good Friday from noon to three.

I had supper all planned and would be able to put food on the table at the usual time. When I arrived, the three Olengers were sitting at the kitchen table. Woody and Ted were poring over what looked like statements of some sort. Sam was leaning on his elbows watching. Ted had a piece of paper in his hand and he said, "What do you think of this one, Sam? Uncle Woody doesn't think it's so hot but I like it."

Sam said, "I don't like it at all. It's not a good thing."

I believe Ted was surprised he had gotten an answer; and more surprised at that response. So he asked, "Well, what do you think about selling this and this to buy that?"

Sam peered at the list Ted indicated. "I don't think so, Uncle Ted. Money is going to be very tight soon. We should keep all we have in a safe place."

Ted and Woody both laughed at Sam's seriousness. Then Woody said, "You know, Ted, none of this stuff is that important. Why don't we hold off for awhile. It won't hurt anything and maybe it'll make Sam feel safer."

Ted agreed and they carefully folded all the papers spread across the kitchen table. Sam had a very unusual look on his face. Sort of a satisfied look.

"Can you stay for supper tonight, Mrs. Willoughby? If you can do up the supper dishes tonight I think we will be okay until Monday." Ted handed the papers to Woody who left the kitchen. "The cannery and wharf are closed for the holiday. You may as well have the weekend off as well."

I was excited about having a Saturday off. I could go into San Luis Obispowith my neighbor and do some shopping. There were some leftovers in the pantry and I was sure that Woody could make do for Saturday. I stayed for supper, did up the dishes and showed Woody what was edible and already cooked. The three of them were on their own for an entire weekend. And I was on my own.

Patricia got back the Monday after Easter. Spring perked along as always. She and Sam spent a lot of time walking and watching the seagulls at the City Pier. I had forgotten all about asking her about Sam and his dreams.

At the end of August Woody took Sam to school and registered him for first grade. Sam was very excited. He was going to learn to read books! I didn't have the heart to tell him that he probably wouldn't get past Dick and Jane in the first grade. But, that is reading, I guess.

Patricia gave her notice. Now that Sam was in school five days a week, she wouldn't be needed. She was going to be married in December. Ted and Woody would take turns getting Sam to school at 7:45, I would meet him at school in the afternoon and walk home with him. I would prepare dinner as usual. Mondays I would come at 7, walk Sam to school and came back to do the laundry and weekly house cleaning and then meet him at school.

Sam asked me one afternoon why I wasn't married. I told him that I had been once but my husband died in a storm at sea. Very politely he asked if I would tell him about the storm. Then he asked if I ever thought of Mr. Willoughby. I said yes, often. But some day I would join him in heaven. Meanwhile, I was happy taking care of him and Ted and Woody. Then he asked how old I was. I told him boys shouldn't ask ladies how old they are. He apologized. And then he said, "Well, don't worry, Mrs. Willoughby, you'll live to be at least 105."

At the time he said it I thought that he was just trying to make up for his unintentional rudeness. But now that I'm 101, I am beginning to wonder if perhaps his declaration wasn't more of a pronouncement. I have thought about this pretty often the last year or so. In all these years I have enjoyed excellent health. My doctor is amazed at how 'robust' I appear at 101. Most people are fragile at 80. I believe that somehow, Sam is responsible for my longevity. Somehow.

In late September, Ted got a call from his stockbroker. That was very unusual. And he must have been working really late as he called just before 6 and he was in New York. The telephone was in the hallway between the living room and the kitchen. I was putting supper on the table and overhead the conversation. At least, Ted's half. Evidently the broker said there was a lot of activity in the market just then and wondered if he'd made any decisions on the recommendations he'd sent months before.

Ted told the broker they had reviewed everything but hadn't made any definite decisions. He'd get back to the broker. But it sounded to me like the broker wanted something more solid and right now. Ted insisted he wasn't ready to give him anything. I left when supper went on the table but I am sure they discussed the call.

The next week or so was pretty hectic at the cannery. They were refitting one line and redoing the employee room. That coupled with the unusually heavy arrival of fishing trawlers didn't allow much time to discuss investments. Or anything else. The broker and the investments were apparently forgotten.

One evening a couple of weeks later, Ted was sitting on the front porch listening to the Philco. I remember it was a Thursday—late October. I was headed home. I had stayed to iron a shirt for Sam for a special play at school the next day.

When I arrived the next morning, Ted and Woody were at the kitchen table. They had already had their breakfast, as usual, but now had spread out all those statements I had seen in the Spring. The radio was blaring. Something had gone terribly wrong with the New York Stock Exchange. They were concerned how badly their investments were being affected. Then they realized—they weren't going to be badly affected at all. After Sam had protested their decisions back on Good Friday, they hadn't made further investments, trades or sold anything.

And since they hadn't had time just a month ago, they still hadn't made any major changes. Some of their stock was falling drastically. And it continued to fall for the next week or so. But when the smoke cleared, they weren't going to be wiped out as many others were. They left the house later than usual shaking their heads. If they hadn't indulged Sam, they would have lost several thousand dollars. The list their broker had sent would have wiped them out.

As I walked Sam to school he asked, "We aren't going to lose too much money, are we, Mrs. Willoughby?"

"I don't think it's going to be too bad. How did you know they shouldn't invest more money?"

"I don't know. I just knew."

Sam was six years old. It was 1929.

The next week a telegram was delivered to the house just before supper time. The brokerage firm was closing. Ted should call immediately regarding his and Woody's accounts. Their broker was no longer with the firm and he should ask for a Mr. Swanson. Ted read the wire to Woody and me. Then he said, "Just imagine how tragic this could have been if we had gone ahead this Spring. We didn't actually listen to Sam but, by indulging him at the time and not doing anything, we didn't have time to go ahead later. Fortunately for us. We have lost a lot but not nearly what we could have."

Woody said, almost as an aside, "Maybe we should pay more attention to his ideas."

Ted looked at him with an odd grimace. "There have been things, haven't there?"

Evidently there were incidents they never mentioned where Sam made one of his proclamations and it panned out. I got my jacket and went home, leaving the three of them at the supper table. I pondered Sam's apparent abilities as I walked. What exactly has he said at home that I hadn't heard about? I wondered what has happened in Sam's life that caused this psychic leaning? First the healing and now this.

Other than the fact Sam was a foundling left on a doorstep, what is different about Sam? I'd known him his entire six years and, other than the terrible bee stings when he was two, his childhood had been unremarkable.

I was so deep in thought that night, I almost passed my own street.

Christmas came and went and soon we were in 1930. The weather was so balmy in March that Ted and Woody decided it would be a good time to repaint the house. Being so close to the ocean, it was really exposed to the salt air. And salt air does a real number on the wood siding. In those days, when you hired something done it was usually done in a very expedient manner—no delays, no postponements, just done.

Neither Woody or Ted were inclined to do it themselves. They had a dozen reasons mainly that they had other duties at the cannery and wharf. But actually they didn't know how to paint a house. They hired a local, Tom Wolcott. He gave them a good price of $300. The house is two stories, well actually a story and a half as the second floor is only over the back half of the house. And it's a good-sized house besides. At that time, $300 was a goodly piece of change but not at all unreasonable.

Tom's boy Dicky, just out of high school, was his only helper. They began by removing whatever paint was still on the house—that took a couple days. The first three days went quite well. As soon as Sam got home from school each day, he would head to a spot in the yard where he could see all the action. He wasn't interested in painting but was interested in how it was done. One afternoon he came into the kitchen where I was preparing supper and said, "I'll bet I could paint a house if I had to do it."

I said, "Oh, really?" Sam was six and a half.

"Yep, you have to scrap off all the old paint so you have a nice smooth surface. I could do that. Then you set up a scaffold and paint the house one section at a time. I could do that."

He finished the milk and cookies I had set out for him. "Yep, I could."

"Well, maybe you will decide to be a house painter when you grow up, Sam."

"Oh, I don't think so. I am going to start working at the wharf when I turn eight. That's the family business. But I could paint a house if I had to."

I wasn't about to argue with him. Frankly, I think he could have painted a house if he wanted. He had been very watchful so far. And, he was a very determined boy.

The next afternoon, the fourth day, Dicky was stepping down a ladder off a scaffold and missed a step. He had nothing in his hands—probably a good thing. But he managed to bang his chin on at least a dozen rungs of the ladder before he hit the ground. Tom hurried down the other ladder at the opposite end of the scaffold but Sam beat him to Dicky.

There was a lot of blood. I was imagining a broken jaw, teeth knocked out, maybe a severed tongue—there was that much blood. I cranked the telephone and asked Central to find Dr. Johnson and send him to the house as soon as possible.

Sam came running in and asked me for a pan of ice chips. "I need it in a hurry, Mrs. Willoughby." I chipped a small pan full, handed him two dish towels and off he ran. I could hear Dicky moaning outside. It didn't sound good.

Dr. Johnson showed up about fifteen minutes later. He and Tom eased Dicky into the back seat of his sedan and they took off for the hospital in San Luis Obispo. Dicky had a dish towel of ice tied around his lower face. Sam came into the house looking very worried. Dr. Johnson had listed Dicky's injuries—almost exactly what I had imagined. Sam said, "I tried to help but Dicky didn't want my help. I packed his face in ice though. At least the blood slowed down."

I put my arm around this six-year old who was trying hard not to cry. Somehow he felt he had failed Dicky. "Sam, you did all you could do. Tom didn't do anything but stand and wring his hands. At least, you did something. If Dicky didn't want your help, that's not your fault."

"I know, Mrs. Willoughby. I just feel I could have made him better. But he called me a creepy little kid and to get away from him."

I hugged him to me. He leaned into me and started to bawl. He sobbed for a good ten minutes. Poor little guy. I just kept hugging him until he came up for air. Then I blew his nose and wiped his face. I don't know if he was crying because he hadn't helped Dicky or if it was because Dicky called him names.

"You're a good boy, Sam. Don't be so hard on yourself. Just trying to do good means a lot." I hugged him again.

I thought that as Sam didn't think he had helped Dicky maybe his 'healing power' or whatever hadn't clicked in. Maybe this incident would make people realize he's not a miracle worker. Maybe.

When Ted and Woody got home for supper, they had already heard about the fall. Tom had sent word he'll be back in the morning to finish up. The house was nearly done. Sam said, "I could finish the house. I know I could."

Woody told him that they had already paid Mr. Wolcott to do the painting so we should let him finish the job. Sam sort of nodded his head. Evidently that made sense to him.

The next day Tom showed up around 7:30. Sam had already left for school. I happened to be at the house to do some cleaning that I'd put off. Tom said that Dicky did have a broken jaw and a broken nose. Dr, Johnson had been concerned about Dicky's tongue as it appeared he had bitten it pretty badly. But once the blood was cleared away, the damage wasn't as severe as he had thought. Sam's ice pack kept the swelling down and stanched the blood flow. I asked him if he would tell Sam that when he got home from school as he had been very upset yesterday. Tom said of course he would. "I have never seen a little kid take charge like that before. He seemed to know just what to do. I just stood there helpless."

Dicky was back helping his Dad in his business in a month or so . . . looking as good as new. I kept thinking that if he would have accepted Sam's help that day, he'd been back to work in a week.

The spring wore on and many days I would find Sam sitting on one of the little benches by the beach path, just watching the ocean. I used to stop by and pick him up at school but he insisted he was old enough to walk home alone. Most days we arrived at the house at about the same time but occasionally he'd be sitting staring at the incoming waves.

Chapter Nine

Shortly before Sam's seventh birthday, school was still in session but it was probably late May, a visitor arrived at the house. I had gotten there a bit earlier than normal as I wanted to roast a larger piece of beef than usual. I hadn't been there half an hour when a long black, very fancy car pulled up to the front gate.

I was in the kitchen but the front door was open and I happened to see it stop. An uniformed driver got out, walked around the car and opened the back door. I wiped my hands on my apron as I started through the house to the door. The woman was beautiful. She was fairly tall, very slender. She was dressed in a tailored suit, a royal blue suit. Her heels tapped, tapped, tapped on the front walk. She knocked very quickly—rap, rap, rap. She must have been in her early 30s. She asked if this was the Olenger house and I admitted it was.

She said she had come to inquire about a baby that the Olengers found on their office doorstep about seven years ago. A baby boy.

I said, "What about him?"

She fumbled about in her small hand bag—looking for a handkerchief perhaps. "May I come in please. I feel so conspicuous standing out here."

Well, la-de-dah, she was conspicuous. What did she expect? I opened the screen door. She seemed to float through the door.

"Does the boy still live here?"

"Yes."

"Is he here now?"

"No, he's in school."

She stood there for a moment. I felt pretty conspicuous in my cotton house dress and flour sack apron. Like a bump on a log. Her hat, shoes, purse and gloves all matched. Around her neck she wore a large sapphire set in a beautiful lacey frame. I had never seen anyone so perfect. Yes, that was what I thought; perfect.

"What does he look like?"

"He's just an average seven-year old. Blond hair, blue eyes, tall for his age. Why do you ask?"

"He's mine." She said it so quietly that if I had been any further away, I wouldn't have heard her. "I left him in a produce crate, nearly seven years ago."

"And what do you want now?" I thought, dear God, she can't want to take him away.

"I want to see him."

"That's all?"

She nodded. I breathed a small sigh of relief. Hopefully that was all she wanted. I realized I wasn't being too hospitable.

"Please sit down, Miss???" I had no clue who she was.

"Davies, Marion Davies. You may have heard of me. I'm an actress—in motion pictures."

Maybe that's why she looked vaguely familiar. I didn't go to motion pictures back then but I had seen movie posters when we went into San Luis Obispo or down to San Francisco. Much later I realized that Sam resembled her quite a bit and that was probably why she looked familiar.

"Motion pictures?"

"Yes, you know, films."

"Why did you leave a baby on the doorstep without a note or anything?" Go ahead Agnes—like a bull in a china shop—no finesse—go for the throat. "Excuse me. I must make a call."

I went to the telephone and rang the cannery. Woody happened to answer instead of the secretary. But I wasn't sure who might be listening, party line you know. "Woody, it's Agnes Willoughby. Would you and or Ted be able to run up to the house for a minute? Yes. It is very important. Yes, if you can both come it would be even better. I have a bit of a situation here."

Situation was right. She seemed to have composed herself by the time I returned. "Would you care for a cup of tea? I called the men who found and have raised that baby. I am sure they would like to hear what you have to say."

She nodded and I went to the kitchen to make tea. I fixed a tray with four cups and went back into the living room. Woody and Ted ran up on the porch. I know they had seen the huge car sitting on the road. When I said I had a situation they probably thought of something concerning Sam but the car would throw them off. Still as they slammed through the door their first question was, "Is something wrong with Sam?" They stopped dead still when they saw the woman on the divan.

I introduced them to Miss Davies. "She says she's Sam's mother."

They stood there with mouths agape. "What? Why are you here now? He's seven. What do you want?" They were indignant. I always thought they'd be happy to find out who Sam's parents were. I suggested they might want to sit down. Hopefully this would be a long story . . . long enough to convince us all she was who she said she was.

She took off her gloves, smoothed her skirt and tried to be totally composed. I could see the nervousness under the surface. She may be a movie star but she was afraid of us, or something. Other than a sapphire bracelet that matched the pendant, she wore no jewelry. No rings on either hand. Her hair covered her ears and I wondered if there were sapphires there too.

"In 1922 I was cast in a lead role in the film "When Knighthood was in Flower". It was a tremendous hit—primarily because a certain California newspaperman poured millions of dollars into the production to showcase my talent.

"This wasn't the type of movie I usually appeared in but my friend was very sure it would be marvelous and would launch my career to new heights. He was right, the film did do well, very well. Sometime after my friend and I began to be a bit more than friends and by February 1923 I was sure I was expecting a child.

"I was afraid to tell my friend, my benefactor, for fear he would drop me or insist I terminate the pregancy. After finishing the film and attending the premier, I told him I really needed some time to rest. Filming had been a great strain. I rented a small house just large enough for my personal maid and me in LaJolla. I thought it was far enough away from him and his castle that I could enjoy some privacy. I rented the cottage under my real name, Marion Cecelia Douras. Davies is my stage name. A few people looked at me as though they thought they knew me but overall I was anonymous. I wore no makeup and after April seldom left the cottage as my pregnancy was becoming rather obvious.

"The cottage was as private as I had hoped. I was far enough from San Simeon that he wouldn't just drop in. But he called weekly and begged me to come back soon. I told him I was exhausted and needed more rest. I was quite fatigued. Finally, I told him I would be back in July. The doctor who was attending me said the child should be born no later than the first week of July. Then I realized there was no way I could show up in San Simeon with a baby.

I was delivered on the fourth of July. Independence Day for me in many ways. I called my benefactor and told him I would be back in a few days. My maid made arrangements to hire a car and driver; someone she trusted. We closed up the cottage in LaJolla and started our trip north.

"My maid and I decided we would leave the child at a church. But they all looked so bleak and cold. We drove north along the coast. I was getting panicked by the time we got to Morro Bay. We hadn't found a place to leave the child that I felt good about. We nearly passed by this little town as it was quite dark by the time we got this far. Then we saw a sign on the highway about the cannery. We figured someone who owned a cannery would be able to properly raise a child. You know, have enough money. And, if they didn't want to keep the child, they'd know what to do with a foundling. We were sure the cannery would be open the next day and there was a light on over the doorway. Somehow, I felt it had been left on deliberately so that I would find it.

"And so, we left the baby on the doorstep of the cannery. Later I checked the ownership of the cannery and decided he was in good hands. I checked public records a number of times in the next year and found a substitute birth certificate had been filed. I knew then the child was not in an orphanage. I have wanted, often, through the years to see what happened to the child. Finally, today, I decided I had to find out now. I am on my way from Los Angeles to San Simeon now and knew that if I didn't stop today, I never would."

Woody was livid. "How much are you worth, Miss Davies? Have you come to reimburse us for raising your child? Do you want to buy our silence? You needn't have bothered to stop today. We had no idea who Sam's parents were and didn't care. Or, are you just trying to salve your conscious self by determining that he's alive and well? Why in God's name would you show up now? He's nearly seven. It's been seven years since you abandoned that child." Woody is the most emotional of the two brothers—at least, he tends to show his emotions more. He held nothing back that afternoon. He was so livid he was shaking. Ted reached over and put his hand on Woody's arm as if to say, 'it's okay, it's okay'.

She began to cry again. "I was twenty-six years old. Certainly old enough to know better. If I had gone to my friend, I am sure he could have arranged something but my religion rebelled against that. Also, I was famous by that time. I had just completed filming the largest movie of my career. I couldn't just show up with a child. The studio would have let me go. My reputation would have been ruined."

"But why now? What is it you want? Do you think we should return Sam to you?" I suddenly realized that Ted was frightened too. I could see that he felt this woman posed a threat to his happy home.

She cried some more. "No, I just want to see him. I've never married. I just want to see him. I just want to see him."

I poured more tea all around. Miss Davies picked up her cup and drank. Her beautiful carefully made up face was blotchy and red. She had two crumpled hankies in one hand. I looked at Ted and Woody and they looked at me. What in the world do we do now? Sam was due home from school any minute. No one said anything. We drank our tea.

A few minutes passed and then the front gate slammed. Sam came racing up the porch steps. "Mrs. Willoughby, did you see that car in front? Wow! It's really a beaut." He slammed into the living room. When he saw the four of us sitting there, he came to an immediate halt and said, "Oh, sorry. I should have known we had company. We don't know anybody with a car like that."

Miss Davies sat her cup down on the saucer. It was slightly tilted. I know she didn't notice. She just stared at Sam. I am sure she was seeing her likeness in him.

Woody said, "Sam, this is our friend Miss Davies. She just stopped by to say hello."

Sam walked right up to her and stuck out his hand. "Glad to meet you Miss Davies. That sure is some car you have."

She smiled. "I am very glad to meet you Sam. Is that your full name?"

"Oh, no ma'am. My full name is Samuel Christian Olenger. I'll be seven years old in forty-two days."

She looked as though she was mentally counting on her fingers. "Yes, the fourth of July. I knew that."

"You did?" Sam looked at her surprised.

"Oh, yes, I've known you since you were a baby. I just haven't been around much because I've been so busy making motion pictures."

"I'm afraid I don't know much about motion pictures, Miss Davies."

"Don't worry, you have plenty of time to learn about them."

She was still holding his hand and he didn't appear the least bothered by it. He took his free hand and patted her arm. I knew that Sam could tell she had been crying and was trying to comfort her. That's how Sam worked. The resemblance between them was quite evident now. The nose, the eyes, there was no doubt in my mind she was his mother.

Woody and Ted sat very quietly. I am not sure if they were afraid she'd tell him the truth or if Sam would divine it.

I poured more tea for our visitor. She released Sam's hand. As she sipped the tea she said, "You have certainly grown since I saw you last. How are you doing in school? What grade are you in?"

Sam chattered away for at least five minutes and she seemed to be taking it all in. She reached out to him with both arms and he just melted into her hug. She hugged him very tightly.

"I am so glad to see you looking so well. When you get a little older, perhaps you will see some of my movies. They're really gown up films so you might want to wait a few years."

Sam nodded but didn't respond otherwise. He just stood in her embrace, very much at ease. Very much typical Sam.

Then she looked at the bracelet, I realized it was a wristwatch, and said, "Oh, I really must be going. My driver wants to be in San Simeon before the evening meal." She released Sam and stood up. He took her hand and looked up at her.

"Thank you so much for coming. It was nice to meet you."

She shook hands all round then and within minutes, she was gone. There was a soft, gentle scent as she moved to the door. I swear it was "Evening in Paris". I had sampled the fragrance once in a department store in San Luis Obispo. The fragrance was as beautiful as she was. It also cost forty dollars a half ounce, even then.

I could tell that Woody and Ted didn't want to say anything in front of Sam. They said they had to get back to the cannery. They looked at me with raised eyebrows. I just nodded. I wouldn't say anything further to Sam either. Sam stood on the porch and watched the limousine turn around and head back toward the highway. He waved and I believe she waved back. The windows were tinted but there seemed to be motion in the back window.

Sam and I went to the kitchen and I poured a glass of milk for him. He sat on the kitchen stool and stacked the cookies I had given him into two piles. After a few minutes he said, "Did you see that car, Mrs. Willoughby? It must have been thirty feet long. And it was so shiny. Wow!"

We discussed the car. I told him I thought it was called a limousine. "Wow! How many people do you suppose can ride in that limousine?" I ventured a guess of eight. "Wow!" That was about the full extent of Sam's curiosity over Miss Davies visit. As usual, he had taken everything at face value.

A few months later a letter from an attorney arrived. Miss Davies had set up a trust fund for Sam so he could go to college if he wanted or whatever. At first, Ted wanted to send the letter back and refuse the trust fund. Woody convinced him that would not be in Sam's best interests. Ted insisted they could give Sam anything he needed, or wanted. They didn't need her money even if she was his mother. Woody agreed but said it was only right to accept the trust in Sam's name. Later, he reasoned, Sam could decide what to do with it. So, eventually, they did intend to tell Sam about his parents—or at least how he came to live here—some day. I don't know if they ever did. I can't recall any further discussion on the matter after that letter arrived.

After that time, I kept track of Marion Davies. By the end of the 1930s her Californian newspaper man was having money trouble and she sold a million dollars worth of her jewelry to keep him afloat. I wondered if the beautiful sapphire pendant was part of that sale. She didn't do any films after 1937. I read that she had a bit of an alcohol problem for a while—one would wonder how much Sam had to do with that. She didn't marry until after her newspaper friend died in 1951. Imagine staying with someone that long without marriage. Maybe it was true love. Whatever it was it was definitely unusual for the time. Personally, I was touched by the way she seemed to try to shield his identity while talking to us that day. She never mentioned him by name, only by occupation. The San Simeon reference only clinched our beliefs. How strange that she would have been so protective of him. She did indicate he was unaware of the pregnancy. Strange. Did she think we were going to tattle on her? Or, perhaps she was afraid we'd try to make a claim for Sam for some of his father's money, or hers. Or, perhaps she was just protective of her reputation. I guess we'll never know what her true intentions were.

She married in 1954, three years after her "friend" had died. She died in 1961. I thought it was a shame that she spent more time as a paramour than as a wife.

It surprised the three of us that Sam never really mentioned Miss Davies again. Once or twice in passing he would mention the car. But he seemed to have no real curiosity about her. Woody wanted to believe that was an indication that Sam wasn't really hers. Ted said she verified Sam was born on the fourth of July. Ted thought she was the real thing. And why would she set up a trust fund if he wasn't hers? And we all had to admit Sam looked a lot like her. We spoke of her only when Sam was not around. But, after a few months, I believe we never mentioned her again. I don't know if Sam thought about her again. I didn't want to ask—maybe he sensed something that afternoon that satisfied him.

And life went on in Cayucos.

Chapter Ten

Sam continued to grow. The next year, when he turned eight, Sam went directly to the cannery after school. He wanted to learn the family business. He was still tall for his age and insisted he was not only tall enough but old enough to work on the cannery lines. Ted figured he could handle the line for the hour left of the shift after Sam arrived from school and finally relented. Because the shift changed an hour after Sam arrived Ted always had something else for him to do. He reminded Sam that he could not leave in the middle of a shift if he was on the line so he couldn't work the second shift. Woody and Ted always left the cannery in time for supper at home. Sam saw the wisdom in working to the end of the day shift and then occupying himself with other concerns until Ted and Woody left for the day. Sam was never one to miss a meal and as his bedtime was before the end of the second shift he relented easily. So long as he was able to work at the family business, he didn't really care what the hours were.

Sam was working three hours a day during the week and five hours on Saturday. He was absolutely ecstatic when he received his first paycheck. Twenty hours times 25 cents an hour. He had a strategy all worked out. Every other check went directly into a bank account. The cannery was paid every other Saturday. He kept two dollars a month for spending money. I don't know what he spent it on.

He did admit he was saving up to buy a car. Both Woody and Ted smiled behind their hands that day. Ted asked, "A car, right, not a limousine?"

Sam said, "What would I do with a limousine, Ted? I want to get one of those Fords."

It was 1932, March, and Sam was 8 years old. Woody called me at home before 6:30am. Sam was sick and Woody felt it would be best not to send him to school even though he had no fever. Sam was complaining of a massive headache. Woody said he'd given him an aspirin an hour before calling me, evidently when Sam first woke up, but the headache was persistent. I said I'd be there as soon as I could. Woody said he'd wait for me.

Sam may be 8 but he's still just a little boy. None of us would have thought of leaving him alone even for an hour especially if he was ill.

When I got there, Sam was in bed. Woody said that Sam had not eaten breakfast with them so I might want to try and feed him something. When I went into Sam's bedroom, I found the shades were drawn and his room was cool and comfortable as well as dark. I asked Sam how he was feeling and he said, "I feel just awful. If only they would lock the window I would feel better." I thought he was delirious and took his temperature again. No fever. His windows were not open and I wondered why he was concerned. He agreed to try and eat some breakfast. I poached one egg and toasted one slice of bread.

"Do you want to come eat in the kitchen?" Sam sat up and held his head.

"My head really hurts, Mrs. Willoughby. But it would be better not to eat in bed. I might get toast crumbs in my sheets."

I smiled. How could an eight-year old be so logical when he didn't feel well? How could an eight-year old be that logical at all? Sam put on his slippers and I helped him into his robe. "It looks like you could use a new robe, Sam. You've nearly outgrown this one."

"I guess so." He shuffled out to the kitchen and dutifully ate his egg and toast. He squinted as if to keep the light at a minimum. I felt sorry for the little guy. There was no doubt he was suffering. His lips were drawn and white as were his knuckles. I think it took every ounce of energy he had to eat. I offered him a glass of milk and he said that half a glass would be enough. He drank it very slowly as if the coolness of the milk pained him somehow.

He went back to bed after he had finished. Then he got up and said, "I should brush my teeth." He brushed his teeth and returned to bed. And he stayed there all day. At dinner time I asked him if he would like a bit of soup. Usually he would ask "what kind?" and be ready to eat regardless of my answer. But today he said, "No, I don't think I want anything. Thank you." He pulled the blankets up around his ears.

Woody called to ask how Sam was feeling and I told him the headache had not subsided. Woody asked, "Do you think we should call the doctor?"

I thought that if he was the same in the morning, than yes, call the doctor. The next day was Wednesday so we would have to keep him out of school another day. Sam had missed so few days of school in his life that you could count them on one hand. This was first time though that he was ill. Other times he had gone with Woody and Ted on buying expeditions for the cannery.

I decided to do some baking while I was there and asked Sam if he'd like to come watch or help. He said he didn't think so. Usually he wanted to clean out the batter left in the bowl when I baked cakes. But not today. Then he added, "If only they would lock the window." I took his temperature again. It was not even a degree higher than it had been that morning. He certainly sounded delusional. I did check his bedroom window again. It was locked. I had no clue what window he was talking about. Instead of cake I decided to bake pies and peanut butter cookies before I started to prepare supper. Usually the aroma of peanut butter cookies baking would bring Sam to the kitchen. Not today.

Woody and Ted had just come home when we heard Sam yelling from his bedroom. We all ran. He was screaming, "Don't take the baby. Put the baby back. You are bad people. Go away. Leave the baby alone." Strange thing though, he was sound asleep.

Ted said, "Let's not wake him. But what could cause that kind of nightmare?" We shook our heads. To our knowledge Sam hasn't been around a baby for quite some time. What kind of dream could have caused this outbreak?

Woody told me that later that evening, after I had gone home, Sam sat bolt right up in bed and stated quite clearly, "The baby is dead. But they don't know that yet. Oh, the poor, poor baby."

The next morning Sam was fine. I had come early in case he was still unwell but he was at the table chattering away at Ted and Woody. Woody told me that Sam had awakened at 6 and sat down at the kitchen table. He was very hungry. No one spoke of his headache and, if I didn't know better, I would guess he had forgotten it already. It was almost as if it hadn't happened. Whenever he had dreams, before this time, he used to regale Ted and Woody with them at breakfast. Today he did not mention having any dreams at all the day or night before.

Ted went into San Luis Obispo a few days later to pick up a part for one of the machines at the cannery and brought home a newspaper. When he laid it on the table for Woody and me to see, his hands were trembling and his face ashen. The headline shouted at us: LINDBERG BABY KIDNAPPED! The article read in part: **March 1, 1932** Tuesday evening:—Betty Gow, and Anne Lindbergh, put twenty-month-old Charles Jr., to bed at eight PM. He was looked in on at nine, and found to be sleeping peacefully.

It was more than two months later before the baby's body was discovered. The coroner said the child had been dead for several weeks; most likely since the night he had been taken.

Sam's ravings made sense now—in a way. How could he have known details of this kidnapping when he was in bed with a severe headache? Reading the article through twice, Ted said, "It's almost as though he was there." Suddenly I was terribly afraid for Sam. I'm not sure why but this was too eerie for me to comprehend. Sam remembered none of it but the three of us did and quite vividly at that. Reading the newspaper account made Sam's rantings make sense . . . or would have if he had been there.

Two years later when the Lindberg trial began, Sam made an announcement at the supper table. "That man on trial is not the man that kidnapped the baby." Woody asked how he knew that for fact and he said, "I just know. He didn't do it."

Woody remarked later that he seemed to remember that Sam had said something in his sleep that indicated he had seen the kidnapper or kidnappers. But did he really know? And how?

As I recall, there has been discussion about Richard Hauptmann's guilt all these years since the trial. But he was found guilty, Strangely enough, Sam didn't remember these episodes. Perhaps that was best. But I've never forgotten.

Ted, Woody and I said that we hoped no other major national tragedy would happen if it was going to affect Sam so badly. Can anyone be that sensitive? That psychic? Woody said the use of the word psychic gave him the creeps. Made him think of a snake oil salesman or a carney come on, not his little boy.

Life went on and we all thought we were raising an unusual little boy. But he went on as he always had; a happy, go-lucky, very carefree kid. Other than the comment at the time of the Lindbergh kidnapping trial, Sam never mentioned the incident. I believe he truly did not remember.

One afternoon shortly after this, I arrived at the house just as Sam was due out of school. Sam showed up a few minutes later with a dog trailing behind him. I asked who the dog belonged to and wasn't Sam going to the cannery as usual. He said, "I was almost to the cannery, you know, following the beach to the where the road cuts down from the highway. There was this dog sitting at the top of the road, like she was waiting for me or something. When she saw me she came flying down the hill as fast as I've ever seen a dog run. It was like she knew me. I can't take her to the cannery so I thought I'd bring her home. Do you think Ted and Woody will let me keep her?"

"What makes you think she doesn't already have a home?"

"I just know, Mrs. Willoughby. She was waiting for me."

I hesitated a long minute and said, "Well, the most they can say is no. Leave her here and go on to work."

Sam turned to the dog, "Mitzi, this is Mrs. Willoughby. You stay with her and I'll be back in a little while." The dog seemed to nod her head. Okay, maybe I was seeing things. She stretched out on the front porch and Sam took off running to the cannery.

It was a few hours later that I heard a deep growl. So deep, I heard it in the kitchen. I hurried to the front door. The dog was sitting at the top of the porch steps and would not let Ted or Woody come into the house. I don't know why Sam was behind them as he usually walks with them on the way home. Ted turned around and asked, "What is this all about, Samuel?"

Sam said, "She found me this afternoon and I brought her home." He turned to the dog and said, "Mitzi, this is Uncle Ted and Uncle Woody. They live here. It's okay to let them in." The dog seemed to nod again and let them pass before she laid down under the porch swing.

"How do you know the dog's name if you just met her today, Sam?"

"Oh, she told me."

And that's how Mitzi became part of the Olenger household.

Sam was a great scrounger. He found things along the coast line and he found things just "laying around" sometimes. He scrounged up some scraps of lumber to build a tree house. Well, not actually a house, more a deck. He built a platform in the tree that housed the wasps that nearly killed him. The tree had been badly burned in an effort to rid it of the insects and when it grew back, the main trunk split into three about 12 feet above the ground. Sam built his observation platform there. He could see for miles up and down the coast as well as miles out to sea. He spent many hours on the platform just observing. He could see the highway, the ocean, the pier, the cannery and quite a bit of the coast line from his perch. He often would come in to watch me make supper and tell me about the pelicans or whatever other water fowl had been about that day. Or he'd tell me how many ships he had counted and which way they were sailing. He knew how many docked at the wharf and which were fishing vessels. He knew the tides; when the high tide would come and when the low tide could be expected. Sam was very much aware of his surroundings. The dog would lay up there on the platform with Sam . . . she never bothered the birds or the squirrels who came to visit. Her presence didn't seem to keep any wild thing away. I was rather surprised at that.

Occasionally Sam would run into the house and say, "Come outside and look, Mrs. Willoughby. You can see from the front gate." I'd follow him out and he'd point out a pod of whales swimming a short distance from the shore. That boy loved whales. During the migration season, Sam would count the number of whales he saw every day and then regale Ted and Woody at supper.

One afternoon as I watched him from the kitchen window I could have sworn he talked to the squirrels that climbed his tree. More than once I've seen a squirrel or two share the small platform with the blond headed boy and the small dog. Birds frequently would stop by as if to rest and visit with Sam for a few minutes. It was quite amazing to watch him.

Once, and only once I believe, he mentioned to me that he had seen a limousine on the highway. "A lot like the one Miss Davies rode in." So, while he wasn't discussing her, he hadn't forgotten her. I read the entertainment news whenever I got a big city newspaper. Miss Davies and Mr. Hearst were fodder for the news media back then. Hollywood was a separate world in those days. The actors seemed more private in their daily lives and avoided the media unless their Studio had set up a camera opportunity. But with Hearst and Miss Davies, it seemed a photographer was sure to be close by. I am grateful that none had followed her here that day when she came to check on Sam. I've wondered many times how she happened to choose the Olenger house to inquire after the infant she had abandoned all those years before. Was it because of the proximity to the cannery when she had deposited the crate with Sam in it? No one in town mentioned her after that day so I believe she didn't stop somewhere and inquire before coming to the Olenger house. Perhaps she had had someone check all that out for her long ago. I know she told us she checked to see if Sam had ever been adopted and by whom but as we didn't really have street addresses then, how did she chose this particular house? Who knows? Yes, she had someone check where the Olengers lived before she came. That was probably the case. She surely would not just go knocking on doors looking for the baby she abandoned so many years before.

But regardless of how she found him, Sam went on as always. He was an adventurer. He was sure he could do anything. He talked to people, animals and birds. That was Sam at eight.

One morning, I arrived at the Olenger house a few minutes earlier than usual. I was surprised, even so, to find them still at the breakfast table. Sam seemed especially happy to see me. "Watch this, Mrs. Willoughby, Mitzi is sure a wonder dog." He held up a pancake and said to the dog, "Would you like another pancake, Mitzi?"

The dog came to him and sat on her back haunches. He held out the pancake and she took it, quite gingerly, in her mouth. Then she went to the kitchen door. Sam let her out and she went carefully down the porch steps. There were a couple of flat rocks next to the steps and she dog gently laid the pancake on a rock. There was not a hole in it—no tooth marks, nothing. Sam said, "Isn't it amazing? She didn't tear the pancake at all."

I watched her for a few minutes before she finally sat down and carefully ate the pancake.

Sam was astonished that a dog with big teeth could carry a pancake so far without damaging it. And, in retrospect, I guess it was quite a feat. The three of them thought it was amazing and had been giving the dog pancakes for several minutes. They had lost track of time and raced out of the house when the wharf whistle blew. Mitzi was right behind them.

It had been a long time since Sam's 'healing powers' had been used—that I knew of. After he was rebuffed by Dicky Wolcott he seemed to change somewhat. He was still a helpful child but didn't rush to help as he once did. I don't know if the power had been dormant or if the psychic thing had superseded the power or maybe it had left him. But one afternoon on the playground it returned.

At recess a classmate was hit squarely in the face by an empty moving swing. Someone had bailed out of it and, on the backswing, it hit Roger Langer. According to reports, Sam was less than twenty feet away from Roger when the swing hit him. Roger was knocked out cold and his nose was bleeding profusely. Sam grabbed him and carried him inside where the teacher applied cold compresses while another child was sent for ice and another for Roger's mother.

By the time Mrs. Langer arrived, Roger was conscious and holding his nose. The teacher was sure it was broken but the ice prevented swelling and the bleeding had stopped. Mrs. Langer stayed at school until Roger was feeling well enough to walk home. He returned to school the next morning sporting two black eyes. He said the Doctor had come and said he was damned lucky not to have a concussion. The teacher was amazed. Not only at Roger's quick recovery but that he didn't have a concussion or a broken nose.

When I heard about it I thought Sam's healing force has returned. Maybe it had never left. I wrote to Patricia, who was then living in Oregon. She said it didn't sound as dramatic as Sam's prior healings so maybe it was nothing after all. In a way, I hoped she was right.

But at Thanksgiving the year Sam was eight, I burned myself badly with boiling water while pouring the water off potatoes to mash for dinner. It hurt so much I was in tears. I could see my skin curling up to fall off my hand. Sam grabbed my hand and held it under the pump while he pumped the clear, cold water. Ted and Woody had asked me to stay for Thanksgiving dinner, as had become our custom over the years.

By the time I put dinner on the table, my hand was nearly back to normal. It was a bit more red than usual and Woody commented on it. I told him I had scalded myself while preparing dinner. He made some comment about fortunately it wasn't too severe. I know how badly burned it was. I saw it. I felt it. I watched my skin crinkle. Sam's powers were still in full effect. But, I now swear by cold water for burns.

We had snow for Christmas that year. And Sam got a sled. He was in seventh heaven. The house is on a slight hill and he found he could coast all the way down to the cannery on his sled. Ted said he'd never seen a kid more enchanted with a sled. He would jump onto the sled and push off. As the sled began to move, Mitzi would leap on top of Sam. It was quite a sight to see sled, boy and dog race down the hill. When the sled came to a stop, Mitzi would get off and wait for Sam to get up and turn it around to go back up the hill. Quite frequently, as soon as he started to pull the sled upward, Mitzi would jump on the sled. She didn't seem to mind if it went fast or slow—she liked riding the sled. Sam didn't mind pulling her uphill. He'd laugh and talk to her all the way up.

As I think back on those Christmases when Sam was a kid, he certainly wasn't spoiled. He received one gift a year for Christmas. And one a year for his birthday. But I don't recall Sam ever thinking he was under privileged. It was sort of the norm to not give children an abundance at holidays. One good gift was sufficient back then.

We never determined for sure what breed Mitzi was. She looked quite a bit like a small coyote—except for her tail. It was plumed and curled over her back. One day while I was baking cookies, Sam and I discussed Mitzi. He announced that she was coyote and Spitz. I never challenged that—he seemed quite sure. I was just as sure if I asked how he knew he'd tell me that Mitzi herself had told him.

Sam loved the ocean. Even when the wind was whipping the sea into 30 foot waves, Sam would stand on the hill by the cannery overlooking the Pacific—hands jammed into his jacket pockets, wind tossing his hair wildly. Remembering my own childhood fantasy with the ocean, I often wondered what he was thinking as he stood there. Some days when I recall him on the hill I wish I had asked what was on his mind as he stood there—often for twenty minutes at a time.

He walked the beach often on his way to school. It wasn't actually on his way but he left the house early enough to take the long route. This early morning beach walking began after Patricia left and he had convinced Ted and Woody that he was capable of walking himself to school. Once Mitzi arrived she walked him to school daily. She would return home after leaving him at school and lounge around the front porch. Sometimes she would sniff out things in the yard. But, at the right time every afternoon, she would leave the yard and return to school to walk Sam home. I was amazed at how she seemed to tell time. She walked him to the cannery on the days he was supposed to work and often waited for him on the path that led up to the house.

Ted and Woody took to Mitzi quicker than I thought they would. Soon she was laying under Sam's chair at the supper table waiting for him to sneak food to her or to clean up whatever he dropped. She rapidly became a member of the family.

Sam never gave up walking the beach as he found things that interested him; mostly junk but, to Sam, interesting junk. He always carried a bag with him so he could stow his treasures until he got home.

On the weekend he would sit on the back porch and go through the things he had gleaned during the week. Mitzi sat on the porch steps and supervised. Well, that's how it looked. He'd hold up an item and say, "What do you think of this, Mitzi? Pretty neat, huh?"

Many a time he'd come into the kitchen to show me some marvelous thing. Shells were the most common thing he found but not all the shells were common. He knew what kind of animal had lived in each shell. Sam found a ring once; onyx set in silver with an initial on the stone. He was fascinated with the way the stone was set and tried to figure how the silver letter W was attached to the stone. After thoroughly examining it, he gave the ring to Woody. Woody was surprised at the gift and felt the ring was rather valuable. He questioned Sam as to where he had found it and when. Finally, he decided it had belonged to a tourist (Sam found it on the public beach) and he could keep it in good conscience. The ring fit him and he began to wear it regularly. Sam was very proud that Woody liked the ring and had accepted it. He had spent a good deal of time cleaning and polishing it.

I do know that Woody put a notice card up at the grocer's in case someone had reported it lost or were looking for it. No response came and after a year he took the card down.

Sam found bicycle chains, automobile parts, reading glasses, unusual stones, a house key and several other pieces of beach debris. He even found a pair of shoes once. He said he left them on the sand for three days and when no one came back for them, he brought them home. Sam would spread out the week's findings on the back porch, clean the sand from everything, try to figure out where each item came from and then put it in a box. By the time he was a teenager, he had a large box full of things he'd found along the shore.

He knew every nook and cranny of the shoreline of Cayucos.

Since then I have wondered often how differently Sam might have been if he hadn't been an only child—an only child raised by two bachelors. He had friends but the relationships seemed different to me somehow. Sam was a good friend and treated his friends well but there seemed to be a personal connection missing. I don't know how to explain it. The type of warmth I enjoyed growing up in my own friendships seemed lacking. It seemed almost as though his relationships were nothing more than superficial, temporary arrangements. There wasn't anyone in particular that he played with or wanted to see on the weekend. His primary objective after school was the 'family business'. He often seemed older than his calendar age. Sam was a serious child most often. He lightened up a bit after Mitzi came but not much. Perhaps it would have been different if Mitzi had appeared earlier in Sam's life.

Sam was an intense boy but that intensity didn't exist outside himself except in his devotion to the ocean, the birds, the marine life and Mitzi. If it hadn't been for that dog I believe he would not have had much of a childhood. Living with two bachelors can be a sobering experience. Mitzi kept reminding him it was time to play, to be a boy. I honestly feel she helped round out his personality.

By the time Sam was ten he was as tall as I was. He was a handsome lad. And smart.

He brought homework home but usually had it completed immediately after dinner. Working at the cannery didn't seem to slow him down at all. He and Woody and Ted would gather around the Philco to listen to "The Shadow", "Sky King", "The Lone Ranger" and whatever other programs they followed. The rule was his homework had to be finished before the radio was turned on. They never missed a program. Sam's homework was always done. A few times during those early years of Sam I had occasion to return to the Olenger house after dinner. I got such a warm feeling when I came in to find two men, a boy and his dog gathered around the radio listening to a favorite program. It was such a homey atmosphere.

It was about this time, Sam began to question the general scheme of things. One afternoon, as he and Mitzi were sitting on the back porch step watching me shell peas, Sam asked me if I believed in God. I told him that I did.

"Well, Mrs. Willoughby," he screwed up his face as if he was trying to decide how to say whatever it was he wanted to say. "Exactly who is God?"

That was not the question I expected.

"Who is God?"

"Yes, exactly who is God?"

It was then I realized that this kid had never gone to Sunday School or church in his entire life. Woody and Ted both believed in a greater being which they called God but couldn't see wasting a couple of hours listening to Parson Mitchell blather on about sin and damnation. Evidently when their mother was alive they both attended church regularly. At the end of every year they sent a check to the church but, as for darkening the church doors themselves, they couldn't be bothered.

Where do you begin when you want to tell a child who God is? I figured the beginning would be best and started by quoting Genesis. Sam sat there and listened carefully. "But, who is God?" The question wasn't answered by beginning at the beginning. I gave the stock answers and he asked unimagined questions. But in the end, Sam came to an understanding of sorts. He pondered over this for several days and often would have another question when he came in from school.

Then, as suddenly as the issue arose, it died. Evidently Sam had satisfied himself as to who God was.

The year Sam was twelve, 1935, he insisted he should quit school and go to work full-time at the wharf. Ted and Woody protested. He couldn't understand why they didn't want him working. He saved his money. He didn't need more education to work the wharf. That was the first, and only, time I saw the three of them at odds. Sam finally agreed he'd stay in school until he was sixteen but he wanted to work full Saturdays at the wharf. He had given up the cannery because he felt he could do better but the wharf was another matter—it was more of a man's job. No one else in town would hire him because he was too young.

Sam argued that there was new equipment on the wharf for unloading ships and he really wanted to learn all about it. Ted was against it. He felt Sam was too young. Woody said he didn't really agree with Sam's working the wharf but he was as big as half the men. Sam promised to be very careful as if that would make them change their minds. Why didn't they give him a chance? Ted said so long as Sam's schoolwork didn't suffer they'd give it a shot. And so, at twelve, he began working ten hours most Saturdays at the wharf. He learned quickly and often had suggestions on how to make some task easier. When new equipment was ordered, he learned everything there was to know about it. He was actually a valuable asset. And, the men seemed to work harder when he was there. It would have been embarrassing to be outworked by a boy. Even a boy as big as Sam.

I was against the ten hour work day on Saturdays. At twelve I felt it was asking too much for a young boy. But he was steadfast and insisted he would cut back or quit when he thought it was too much. To my surprise both Ted and Woody agreed. I am sure they both thought he'd soon tire of the ten hour work day. But it didn't happen.

One Saturday afternoon half the crew was sitting on the pier eating lunch. The Saturday crew ate in two shifts so someone was always available if a ship docked. It was a beautiful summer day and everyone was in a great mood. One of the men had brought a block of cheese but when it came time to eat, he couldn't find his knife. One of the others said, "Here, use mine." He flipped an open knife to his co-worker—who missed the handle and grabbed the blade. There was blood everywhere. The man kept screaming that his fingers were cut off. Sam laid down his lunch, took his handkerchief from his pocket and wrapped the hand and fingers as tightly as he could. He asked someone to fetch the doctor. Everyone was standing around gawking and Sam had to yell. "Go get Ted. Get some help. Now."

Woody happened to step outside just at that moment and came running. He took one look at the worker's hand and blanched. He added his handkerchief to Sam's already blood soaked one and then hustled the man into the wharf's old truck. The man was fading rapidly and Woody yelled, "Sam, come help John sit up so I can get him to the doctor."

Sam climbed into the cab and crouched on the floorboard so he could hold John's hand above his head. Woody said maybe that would slow down the bleeding. Woody said Sam was all folded up under the dash but he kept talking to John the entire time. Sam was now covered with the man's blood but he still crooned to his injured co-worker. It took nearly ten minutes to get to Dr. Johnson's office. Fortunately, he was in. Woody put his arm around John and helped him into the office. Sam sat down on the running board. Woody said he looked positively washed out.

Mitzi had been sitting in the same spot all the while they were gone. When they returned to the wharf and Sam got out of the truck and sat down, she ran to him and put her front paws on his shoulders. She nuzzled his face and ears looking as though she was whispering words of encouragement to him. He hugged the dog using her as a prop. He was so tired.

Woody tried to convince John to go on home but John said he felt fine and wanted to finish his shift. Sam, on the other hand, went home. I was there when he arrived. Mitzi was walking so close to Sam that his hand brushed the tips of her ears as he walked. I believe she would have carried him if she could have.

"What in the world happened to you, Sam?" His shirt was soaked in John's blood. His hair was matted and he was very, very pale.

Sam grinned. "You know, Mrs. Willoughby, I guess the sight of blood gave me a queasy stomach." I asked him what had happened and he told me. I suggested he go lie down for a while. I took his shirt and put it to soak in cold water. He was so pale. I washed his face and he barely whispered "thank you". Mitzi laid on the end of the bed—I had never seen her on his bed before. She had a rug at the side of his bed where she usually slept.

When Woody and Ted came home, Woody asked how Sam was. I told him he was totally exhausted. Woody said that when the doctor unwrapped John's hand it looked as though the fingers were already beginning to heal. They looked at each other. Ted shook his head. "It's back."

I asked, "Are you sure it was ever gone?" We all shook our heads. Evidently the 'power' is stronger now that he's older but also more tiring for Sam.

Woody was upset. "I didn't think about Sam's powers when I asked him to help me with John. Oh, my god, I didn't think. I just knew he would help and I knew I would need help. Everyone was standing around looking helpless. Sam was the only one that seemed aware of what was happening. I didn't think."

It wasn't until then that I realized that both Woody and Ted had been aware of Sam's 'other side' all along. They just hadn't wanted to admit it out loud. How I wished I had known before that they knew. There were so many times I wanted to say something to them but refrained as I was sure they would say I was crazy.

Sam slept most of that day and very late on Sunday. "It" was definitely back. Mitzi laid on the floor next to his bed after that first day and refused to leave until he was up and about. Periodically, she would stand up at the edge of the bed and nuzzle Sam's sleeping body. Woody said he'd never seen anything like it before—it was as though the dog was playing nursemaid.

The following Saturday Sam got some ribbing from the other wharf workers about his 'weak stomach'. But it was good natured teasing and Sam just laughed it off. John cornered Sam at the end of the shift to say thank you. "Doc says if you hadn't held my hand above my heart, I could have bled to death."

Sam said that he was just following orders—doing what Woody had told him to do. John said, "Yeah, sure. Thanks anyhow." I am sure that John was aware more had happened that day than either of them was letting on.

That year Sam received a bicycle for Christmas. Compared to today's sleek, lightweight bikes, it was a dinosaur. The bike must have weighed fifty pounds. There was a rack on the back and a light front and back; the lights were operated by some gizmo that charged itself as Sam pedaled. It was a wonder for the day and Sam loved it. Whenever he had more than an hour of free time, usually Sunday afternoons, he'd pack a sandwich and something for Mitzi and take off. I saw him cruise through town a number of times. He mounted a crate on the rack for Mitzi and put a small basket on the front handlebars to hold things. Once he stopped at my house and talked for a few minutes. I saw his and Mitzi's lunch, a bowl probably for water for the dog and a camera in the basket. He told me he was going down coast a bit. I wondered what was down the coast that wasn't right here in Cayucos but didn't ask him.

One afternoon he arrived home from school and sat on the kitchen stool watching me finish up supper preparations. Mitzi was laying wound around the stool. Usually Sam would coax a cookie and some milk from me even though supper would be on the table within the hour. That day was no exception. He told me that he had been biking down to Los Osos to watch the birds. He said there was a road south out of Los Osos that ended on the top of a bluff. The birds seemed to congregate in the little cove there. Once he had seen pelicans—fifty or sixty of them. Did I know how big a pelican with spread wings looked in flight? Of course, I didn't so he proceeded to tell me. He described other birds that flocked there. He said the flocking seemed to be one species at a time. Once he saw more than a hundred birds swooping from the level of the bluff down to the ocean below. He had taken some pictures. I asked if I could see them and he went up to his room returning with a good size box of photographs. I was amazed at the clarity and sharpness of the pictures. A Brownie was a cheap camera and not especially good back then. But Sam's photos were amazing. One appeared as if he had been within ten feet of the swooping bird. Sam was very interested in wildlife—sea birds in particular. It is regretful that his photos were not in color. But color photos weren't readily processed back in the mid-thirties. The average man shot black and white. And Sam's black and white photos were, and still are, some of the best I have ever seen. He was the Ansel Adams of birds. Well, that is my personal opinion. I have kept all of Sam's photos. I should really do an exhibition some day. I believe people would be amazed.

When Sam was 13, he came home from school and complained of a bitter headache. The only other time I had known him to have a fierce headache was the Lindberg baby episode. I wondered, to myself, what sort of disaster was going to happen. I mentioned to Woody that evening as I dished up supper that Sam was suffering another bad headache. He said, quietly, "Mark the date down somewhere. He may be ill but this may be another one of "those" episodes."

So I marked down the date, May 6, 1937. A few weeks later Ted went to San Francisco to pick up parts for the cannery line sealing machine. He brought home a newspaper and showed it to Woody who saved it for me. The headline was simple: HINDENBURG BURNS MANY DEAD

"The dirigible **Hindenburg** destroyed on Thursday 6 May 1937 as the LZ 129 Hindenburg caught fire and was consumed within one minute while attempting to dock with its mooring mast at the Lakehurst Naval Air Station which is located adjacent to the borough of Lakehurst New Jersey. Of the 97 people on board, 35 people died in addition to one fatality on the ground. The actual cause of the fire remains unknown, although a variety of theories have been put forward for both the cause of ignition and the initial fuel for the ensuing fire."

There were a few photos. I read the full article and came back to the date. I shivered involuntarily. Woody took the paper from me. "Do you think we should show this one to Sam?" We had kept the Lindberg newspaper from him.

I shook my head. "No. I don't think we should show him. He's 13—that's enough to worry about." Ted agreed and Woody took the newspaper and hid it in one of his dresser drawers, with the other.

A few months later, just before the company picnic and Sam's birthday, he seemed to be extraordinarily interested in airplanes. He asked everyone he came in contact with whether or not they had even been in an airplane. He asked me if I had any idea why it was that women didn't get to do the kind of things that men do; like fly airplanes. I told him that some women did fly airplanes and mentioned Amelia Earhart. He said something very odd. "Yes, but it is important to return from your flight if you want to promote flying for women."

I puzzled over that and asked him what he meant. He said he wasn't sure. "But if a woman wanted to do something that usually only men did, she has to do it better and then tell everyone about it."

That made sense to me. It did then and it still does.

When the butcher brought the pigs for the bar-b-que, he also brought several newspapers with him. We didn't have a newspaper in Cayucos or newspaper delivery so didn't keep up with anything that wasn't on the radio. And there weren't six hours of news on the radio every day so we seldom heard the world news. Of course, the few days before the big company picnic, I doubt that any of us had time to turn on the Philco and listen to just the news. If we had, we would have known that Amelia Earhart had gone missing on July 2nd during her planned flight around the world. Sam didn't have nightmares just images. And he talked about those; airplanes, airplanes, airplanes. The headlines were bigger than when the Lindberg baby was kidnapped. A woman flying around the world was evidently a big deal. EARHART LOST ?????

Woody added that newspaper to his dresser drawer. We didn't mention the story to Sam but I believe that somehow he knew. Maybe not the exact details but he knew Amelia Earhart was lost. He had to have known to tell me what he had about women doing things better and then telling everyone about them.

I realize that most of my memories about Sam are eerie—at least, as I recall them now it seems so. Sam actually was a normal everyday kid—until something odd happened. He continued to grow and was soon taller than both Woody and Ted by several inches. With his blond hair, sparkling blue eyes and perfect teeth, he was really quite a handsome sight. Many of the girls thought he was just 'wonderful' but Sam didn't seem interested much in girls. And they knew it. However that didn't keep them from looking at him with a sigh. I actually saw that happen more than once when he went with me to buy groceries.

But when Sam was fifteen, he fell in love. Madly, deeply, irrationally in love. He had promised to stay in school until he was sixteen and suddenly he was glad he made that promise. He met Emily Purcell in school. Her family had moved to Cayucos at the beginning of the school year.

Emily was a petite, blue-eyed blonde. They were a handsome couple. He walked her home after school every afternoon before going to work. He left home early every morning to walk her to school. Mitzi never relinquished her job as guardian and walked with them both ways. Emily was fourteen. They spent a lot of time together. When Ted asked him about his intentions he said that Emily insisted she finish high school before getting too serious. Ted said he thought that was a very sound approach. I think Ted was hoping she'd convince Sam to stay in school as well. But Sam was stubborn—he'd made up his mind he was going into the family business and didn't need school after he was sixteen.

But Emily had dreams of leaving Cayucos after graduation. Sam tried, without finesse, to convince her that Cayucos was a fine town. Her family had lived in San Francisco for several years when she was younger and she liked the big city. She missed the atmosphere, all the things to do, places to go. Sam asked why they had moved here and she said that some relative had died and left the farm to her Dad. He had recently lost his job in San Francisco and there was no choice but to move to the farm. There'd be no rent and maybe he could find a job. Her Mother wasn't over thrilled with the move as she suddenly became a home gardener. And she wasn't too pleased with such a big house; and she missed her friends. I don't know if it rubbed off on Emily or if Emily actually preferred the big city. Do you really know what you prefer at fourteen?

After the first few weeks though, Mitzi did stop going with Sam when she knew Sam was going to be with Emily. Mitzi actually growled at Emily a few times. Woody thought it might be jealousy. Ted opined that maybe she just didn't like Emily once she got to know her. Either way, when Sam was with Emily, Mitzi was on the front porch, watching the path. The moment she saw Sam, without Emily, she'd run down the walk to meet him. If the gate was closed, she sometimes vaulted right over it. Sam would kneel down, scratch her ears and talk to her in a low, quiet voice. Mitzi was happiest when she was with Sam.

Ted and Woody were aware that Sam was spending more time away from home than ever before. So when Sam brought Emily around to meet them, finally, they weren't too surprised. What did surprise me was neither of them thought too much of Emily. They didn't dislike her but they didn't like her, either. As Woody said, "There's something about that girl that I don't trust."

They were surprised when they learned (and I am not sure how this happened) that Sam wasn't putting any money in the bank—even though he was working at least twenty-five hours each pay period.

Finally Woody couldn't take it any longer—knowing Sam was spending money—and he confronted Sam just before supper one evening. Sam had come slamming into the house not ten minutes before he knew they would be sitting down to eat. I was still there, putting the food on the table and doing general clean up. It was the first time I had heard Woody speak to Sam in such a manner.

Woody asked Sam if he had decided not to buy a car after all. Sam asked, "What do you mean?" Woody said he understood that Sam had quit putting money into his bank account. Sam looked rather sheepish and said, "Well, I have been spending money a bit lately. I think I have enough for a car already."

"Sam, that's a lot of money to be spending. May I ask what you're doing with it?"

Sam looked Woody square in the eye and said, "No, you may not." He went out to the back porch and washed up for supper. Woody was left standing in the kitchen—he looked rather dazed. Indeed, I felt rather dazed myself. Sam came back into the kitchen and sat down at his usual place. Woody stood there for another minute or so and then sat down. I finished putting supper on the table and picked up my sweater. Rudeness had never been a part of Sam's personality before. And his response and attitude was definitely rude. This was a side of Sam none of us had ever seen. I realize now that we were lucky. Fifteen year olds are frequently rude. We didn't know that as none of us had raised a child before.

As I passed through the living room I told Ted supper was on the table and I'd see him tomorrow. I should have warned him there was a small storm brewing in the kitchen but I was a coward. I also felt it really was none of my business. Ted should have realized something was amiss as Mitzi was sitting, almost at attention just outside the dining room doorway. She stayed out of family feuds.

Well, as you may have guessed. Sam was trying to buy Emily's interest. He wanted her to forget about leaving town when she graduated. Later he talked to me about it and said, "I don't see where I was doing anything wrong. I just wanted Emily to see there are good things in Cayucos."

"Sam, she's fourteen. She's a freshman. It'll be three years before she actually makes a decision to leave. Why don't you just turn on the Ole Sam charm and hope for the best? Buying her things isn't going to do it. She'll hate leaving you but she'll still leave Cayucos . . . unless you can change her mind with your wit, your charm, your loving self."

He sat on the kitchen stool eating cookies. "You're probably right, Mrs. Willoughby."

Sam was always upbeat but there were times I could tell he was having "Emily" trouble. He'd mope about a bit and ask nonsense questions not even listening to my answers. Inevitably I'd say something about "and how is Emily?". He would groan a little and remark that things were the "same old, same old" with Emily. It must have been hard to understand a young girl who probably had no clue what she really wanted, other than out of town. Sam pretty well took Emily in stride. He so wanted to convince her how great Cayucos was but had no true way to do so. He did agree to stop trying to buy her interest. In fact, he seemed rather relieved after that decision was made. I said once that when you had to buy someone's interest it was actually like pounding sand down a rat hole. He looked at me a bit doubtfully at that time but later he said, "You know, you're right. Even if you give someone something to see things your way it doesn't mean that they do or that they ever will. It is like giving money away."

Sam had been sincere when he said he thought he had enough money to buy a car and soon after began "researching". Of course, Emily was interested in a car. So was every other person in the school. No student owned a car and only a few of the teachers did.

On his 16th birthday, during the company picnic, he talked to everyone that owned a car, had ever owned a car or had even ridden in one. He wanted details about cost, upkeep and, of course, speed. The next day he asked Ted to take him to San Luis Obispo to buy a car. So on a Tuesday, or perhaps it was a Wednesday, after Sam's birthday, Ted and Woody took off early from work and the three of them, and Mitzi, went to look at cars. 1939 was a good year for cars; at least Sam thought so. All he talked about that week was cars; especially Fords, the 1939 models.

They looked at the new cars on the lot first and Sam fell in love with the 1939 Ford Deluxe. For the first time Ford had put hydraulic brakes on a car. Plymouth and Chevrolet had had hydraulic brakes for a long time, Sam told me. But 1939 was the first year Ford put the "juice brakes" on one of their models. Sam sounded more like the salesman than the salesman according to Woody. He hadn't missed a detail apparently as the salesman just nodded as Sam talked.

But the hydraulic brake wasn't the only new feature. Sam had a brochure. The frontal area of the radiator was increased for better cooling. The engine was conservatively rated at 85hp and was updated with larger bearings and a heavier crankshaft that now drove the engine fan. And the new style seats had deeper springs. Oh, yes, Sam knew all about this car. However, the base price was $742. Even Sam thought that was a bit steep for an automobile. He said, "I've got that much money but I believe it is entirely too much to spend for an automobile, even a Ford."

They looked at used cars on the lot and found a 1932 Model 18; deuce coupe. The "1" stood for first and the "8" for V-8. It was different in a lot of ways—the gas tank had been relocated from the cowl to the rear of the car and could no longer rely on gravity feed so a boss fuel pump was added as well as a larger counter balanced crankshaft, pressurized camshaft and main bearings and an improved water pump. It had three windows and front-opening doors. Sam confided that the salesman had called them "Suicide Doors". The price was $490.

The salesman was a bit upset, Sam said, when he opened the driver's door to demonstrate something to Sam and found Mitzi sitting in the passenger seat. No one knew how, or when, the dog got into the car but there she was. The salesman sputtered and Sam said, "That clinches it. This is the car for me." He got into the driver's seat and leaned back with a large sigh. Then he reached over and scratched Mitzi's ears. "This is a pretty nice car, hey girl?" Mitzi gave one bark.

Ted put a deposit down to hold the car until Sam could go to the bank and get the funds needed to buy the car. The dealer was willing to take a handshake but Ted insisted. He wanted Sam to do business the proper way. Sam had been saving since he was eight. Back then, interest rates were very generous and Sam's eight years of saving had given him more than enough to buy the car.

Sam also bought several gas cans from the dealer. We didn't have a filling station at that time in Cayucos. It was not until 1942 that a station opened in town although there was one at Cambria, Morro Bay and, of course, San Luis Obispo. But Sam figured it was much better to have fuel on hand when you needed it. There was a small shed next to the house where he stored his extra fuel. It wasn't airtight so fumes never built up. Sam was concerned about safety too.

The purchase of the coupe began the period of late night Saturday nights. Supper was no later than 6; Sam would pick Emily up by 7 and they would go to San Luis Obispo to see the motion pictures. Emily had an eleven o'clock curfew which Sam said made it a big rush to get home. After the picture show they usually would stop in a malt shop in San Luis Obispo for a soda before coming home. Sam kept very close watch on the time as he knew the first time Emily missed curfew would be the last time she could go out with him for a long while. Her Dad was working at the prison in Atasadero as a guard or something and he scared the bejebbers out of Sam. Sam said Emily's Dad was a nice man but when he was in uniform he looked ten times bigger than when he was in civies. And it seemed that Emily's curfew had been set so that she would be home by the time her Dad left for work. So he was always in uniform when Sam saw him.

Frequently Sam and Emily went driving on Sunday afternoons. Emily's family went to church and Sam would have to wait until afternoon to pick her up. Sometimes on Saturday he'd ask if I could set aside something he could take as a snack on their Sunday rides. Sometimes Emily brought something. Mitzi hated those Sundays. At least, Woody thought so. The dog didn't care for Emily and, even though Sam invited Mitzi to come along, she would not spend time with Emily.

One Sunday they drove down to Los Osos for a circus. Emily's Sunday curfew was nine because of school the next day. Sam reported to me on Monday that they almost didn't make it back in time as there had been an accident on the highway and it took a while to get around it. I reminded him that he should make allowances for such road problems. He agreed I was probably right but I don't know that he ever did. He wanted to spend every waking minute he wasn't working with Emily. Mitzi suffered badly during this period. She wasn't much of a moper but would stay on the porch, head on her paws, waiting patiently for the little deuce coupe to come chugging up the lane. I was surprised that Sam wasn't more tuned into Mitzi's misery.

And so, life went on in Cayucos.

Chapter Eleven

Sam turned eighteen on July 4, 1941. He had worked his way up at the wharf to unloading foreman. No one resented him; he had come by the job the hard way; he earned it. He was still a tall boy; taller than most his age at that time. I see very tall boys a lot these days but in 1941 the average height was less than six feet. He had a boyish face but still carried himself as a person much older than his 18 years. New employees always called him Sir; that may have been because of his name but he did look old enough to command respect. His work also commanded respect. No one could ever say he didn't pull his weight on the wharf. And he was always johnny-on-the-spot when they needed help of any kind in the cannery. He knew the equipment as well as Ted or Woody. Maybe better. No matter what had to be done on the wharf, he was up to it. And he always seemed to know what had to be done. Woody said Sam seemed to have a natural talent for the job. Woody said there were many times he wished his father could have known Sam. In so many ways, Sam was like the elder Sam Olenger—good work ethic, honest, caring, ready to do what was right. Sam wore the name well.

Emily started her senior year of high school in the fall of 1941. Even by that time she had not reconciled herself to living in Cayucos; even with Sam. Still, they were together constantly and everyone expected they would marry as soon as she graduated. She made no bones about wanting to leave town. Sam said she didn't mention it often but some evenings when they were just hanging out she would 'say things'. Sam confided that he had no intention of ever leaving Cayucos so she would have to change her mind. Emily would sort of 'sniff' at that but seldom said anything. He said that, at those moments, he had the feeling if he wanted to marry Emily and live with her, he was the one that would have to change his mind. She was quite steadfast to the idea of getting out of Cayucos as soon as she could. I am sure she felt that if Sam would change his mind, they could leave at any time as he was a "provider" and she needed someone to provide for her until she could put roots down elsewhere. They both were stubborn and I was positive they would never marry.

Sam, on the other hand, hoped for the best and was saving to buy a ring.

And then came December 7, 1941; Pearl Harbor. About one-third of the boys working at the cannery and the wharf immediately went down to San Luis Obispo to enlist in the military—Sam was among them. He had been having nightmares for several nights before the attack on Pearl Harbor and mentioned some of them to Woody as they walked to work that week. He talked about large ships ablaze; sinking into a harbor. He mentioned dive-bombing planes that seem to come directly from the sun—they looked like the sun to him but a sun with wings. Woody asked if it was our harbor that the ships were sinking into and Sam said that he didn't recognize it. Where ever it was, it was more populated than Cayucos. Woody mentioned these discussions to Ted and me one evening. He said Sam told him it was like watching a movie. And it was frightening.

When the attack was announced on radio that Sunday morning, Woody knew that Sam's nightmares had been omens. Even that part of his 'power' seemed to be enhanced as he got older. Not surprisingly, Sam said he was going to join the Army.

Sam had no illusions about war and possibly not coming home. He told Woody and Ted that he was going to write a will so that he could be sure his share of everything stayed in the family. Both of them thought that was an excellent idea and the three of them went to see their attorney and have wills drawn up. The wills were simple—each left everything to the other two and in the event the other two should have predeceased him, everything was left to me. I protested saying that I, being the oldest, would surely be the first to leave the planet. Ted said, "We have to leave it to someone and the courts won't recognize Mitzi Dog."

Truthfully, I was surprised that Sam had a share of everything. I realized I didn't know everything that went on at the Olenger house. But Ted and Woody had incorporated the business many years before and when they realized Sam was going to be there, working alongside them, they had written him into the business somehow. I vaguely remember a discussion once where Ted and Woody were thinking about renaming the business to include Sam's name. Sam said it wasn't necessary and the discussion was shelved.

Within two months, one cannery line was closed. Too many of the workers were now in the Army. But not Sam. Sam couldn't pass the physical. We all were amazed. Sam was a healthy specimen; how could he possibly fail the physical? The Army said he was color-blind and he had acknowledged on his application that he was allergic to bee sting.

Sam was totally bummed out. He went back to the recruiting office with the letter in hand. What difference did it make if he was color blind? Evidently he had been all his life and it had never bothered him. Made no difference; if the Army doctor says you're color blind, you're color-blind and you do not get into the Army, or the Navy or any other branch of the military.

It was a hard blow for Sam to take. So many of his friends and co-workers from the Wharf had been accepted immediately. He was just about the only able body male left, not only on the wharf, but in town. So many people made comments about Sam not being in the military that he started carrying the rejection letter around in his wallet.

A few older men were still at the wharf but it seemed everyone had gotten into the military or was otherwise working in what was called the "war effort". Within months various factories converted to "war effort" goods and hired nearly everyone who applied. There wasn't much in the way of "war effort" that the wharf could provide. But Sam stuck with it as it was an important and viable part of the community.

After thinking about it, I decided that Sam's inability to pass the physical was the best thing that could have happened to him. With Sam's healing powers, he would have killed himself from exhaustion trying to save wounded comrades around him. He wouldn't have survived combat more than a week. He would have 'healed' himself to death. I mentioned this to Woody one evening and he was horrified—he agreed. He hadn't thought of that but agreed it was indeed fortunate Sam hadn't been accepted in the military. He was going to say something to Sam to that effect but Ted put the kabash on the idea. First of all, Ted didn't want Sam to know what we knew. I thought that was rather silly as Sam had to know we were aware of his "powers". And secondly, Ted felt that Sam felt bad enough not being accepted; he'd feel really bad if he realized he wouldn't be there to help a comrade. Woody and I could agree with that and so nothing was said to Sam.

Mitzi had been a close companion since day one but her vigilance took on new fervor after Sam's disappointment. She no longer came home after walking the 3 Olengers to work. She stayed on the wharf watching Sam. She found a shaded corner on the inner dock that was out of the way but she could see Sam most of the time. In her best doggie way, she was trying to comfort him.

Then Sam's ego got another crushing blow on Valentine's Day. Sam had bought tickets for the Sweetheart dance in San Luis Obispo. Emily was delighted to go saying she could get a new dress. He planned to ask Emily to marry him after the dance when he took her home. But, at the end of the evening, Emily gave him a letter when they were parked in front of her home. He said he had his hand in his pocket ready to pull out the ring when she gave him the letter. She had the gall to ask him to wait until he got home to read the letter but Sam insisted on reading it then and there. It said that she was no longer interested in seeing him. He could not believe it. They had dated exclusively for more than three years. He wasn't interested in anyone else; how could she be? And why did she wait until after they had celebrated Valentine's Day. He gave her a very expensive heart pendant—which she accepted and kept. Sam was crushed and didn't understand what had happened. Three years is a long time. A long time. He asked her only one question that night. "Did you agree to go with me to the dance just so you could get a new dress?" She refused to answer.

It wasn't until later that he got angry when he realized how she had played him all evening. "Emily played me like a fiddle", he said. And he was dancing to her tune all evening until she was tired of playing. She took his gifts and made a fool of him. And she refused to discuss the letter with him. He was very angry—I thought he was crying as he stomped out of the kitchen. Mitzi was right behind him. Later I peeked into his room—hoping he was not still crying. Sam was sitting on the floor, leaning against his bed. Mitzi was leaning against Sam with a paw on his leg. Sam was no longer crying but was telling Mitzi all about his troubles with Emily. He had one arm around the dog and was stroking her ears as he spoke. I felt so bad for him at that moment. And so glad that he had someone to talk with.

Apparently, Emily could be interested in someone else—someone who wore a uniform. She had been writing to Donny Wolcott who was in the Army. (Donny was Dicky's youngest brother.) Donny didn't feel right that she was seeing Sam and writing to him. She preferred to write to Donny and have a long distance relationship than date someone who couldn't even get into the service. And as crude as that sounds, that is almost exactly what the letter said.

Sam was devastated. Ted and Woody couldn't believe it—even after Sam showed them the letter Emily had written to him. She didn't have the nerve to cut it off by talking it over with him. Woody expounded for days about women who take advantage of a man's good nature. I agreed with him that it was pretty low of her to accept Sam's invitation to a dance and party for the evening and then give him a letter after he got her home. She had carried it with her all evening. She accepted his expensive gift at dinner. Woody wanted to give her a piece of his mind—try to instill some civility into her. Ted said to let it go; nothing would help. Woody thought it would at least shame her but Ted insisted, "Let it go. It's Sam's problem."

Against Woody's best judgment he agreed to let Sam handle it. But he was fuming mad.

I know that it was an expensive evening. Sam had confided in me that he had ordered the tickets weeks ahead to be sure they could get in. In 1942, $50 for a Valentine's Day party was pricey. Sam said it would be worth it as there was a good band for dancing and dinner was included. There was a rose for every lady and candy too. Plus what he had paid for the pendant, he had spent a lot. He never said anything to the guys at work though a couple asked him if he was still seeing Emily. He didn't take her for long drives on Sunday anymore and his friends had noticed. He finally came up with the answer that she was, after all, too immature. I am sure everyone wondered why it had taken three years for him to discover that—and probably wondered how he had discovered it. But Sam had his pride and never discussed Emily beyond that.

Sam was the youngest man at the wharf and cannery for the next two years. One by one the boys came home and returned to work. Woody and Ted were grateful that they had wanted to come back to the Wharf and tried to accommodate their various disabilities suffered in the War. And many of them had disabilities. But they were still willing and able to work. Sam said that a few of them told him he was damn lucky he was color blind. And, after seeing some of them, I agreed. A few missing legs, missing arms. and in some cases, minds. It was tragic to see young men return so debilitated. Sam anguished over his friends' missing limbs and their inabilities to do things they used to do. He once told Woody, "If I'd been there, maybe I could have helped." Woody said he absolutely went cold when Sam said that.

And then, as Woody put it, Emily got her just dues. Woody wanted to call her and gloat but acknowledged that was his most infantile idea in a long time. He just gloated at home. We all did to some extent, I think. Emily deserved what she got—no doubt.

Donny came home with a German war bride. In two years of correspondence, Donny had not mentioned Elisabet. Such a hypocrite! Emily shouldn't be seeing Sam but he was seriously involved in Germany.

Emily moved to San Francisco the fall of 1942 and expected Donny to come home to her there. Her family was still in Cayucos. She had found a job in a dress factory—modeling as well as sewing. Her mother had told Central that the money was not so great but she had a small loft and planned to move to something bigger when Donny came home. He maintained correspondence with her up to the week before his return to the States. How could he not have told her that he had married someone in Germany? It took some doing to get military permission. It wasn't as though he had eloped at the last minute. But, he never mentioned Elisabet. We all wondered how he hid Emily's letters from his new wife.

Her family must have written Emily or called her when Donny and wife arrived in town. The week after Donny's return, Emily came to Cayucos to visit her family. But the first thing she did was find Donny. He happened to be at the Old Pub drinking with friends. This is all hearsay, mind you, but we heard that she walked into the bar, walked up to Donny, called him a few choice names, slapped him in the face, turned and walked out.

Everyone thought that Sam would seek out Emily while she was in town. Sam told me that he had said, "Do you think I am desperate? Or crazy? Emily made her choice and now she is stuck with it." But it was Emily who did the seeking out. She called Sam at home twice that week she was in town and was told he was 'not available'. I could see the turmoil that was churning Sam's mind. He hadn't taken up with anyone else after Emily left. He told Woody it takes a long time to rebuild trust in people. Besides, he had loved her dearly and she walked away from that. He had no desire to even see her again let alone speak with her.

Ted and Woody were proud of the way Sam had handled the entire Emily thing. They just hoped that he hadn't lost trust in everyone.

Chapter Twelve

By 1944 the TWO Wharf and Cannery was booming again. Sam was now foreman of the entire Wharf operation. Ted and Woody were on premises every day but it was pretty much all Sam. He made final decisions though they all discussed them beforehand. Ted and Woody still did the hiring but Sam had firing abilities. He seldom used it but he could have let the whole place go if he wanted.

The company had grown and the annual picnic was the biggest and best ever. The Olenger back yard is at least half an acre of lawn. It was filled with families in 1944. The bar-b-que pit was three times the size of the first one, nearly twenty years before. There were several employees who were at the first bar-b-que and a few teased Sam. He had been such a cute little boy. Sam was 21 that day in 1944. He took the ribbing well knowing it was good-natured teasing. He took pride in the fact that there were employees who had been with the company so long. That meant it was a good company.

That picnic was especially nice. Sam met a girl that he really liked. Rachel's father worked at the wharf and had for four or five years. Rachel graduated high school and went away to school at UC Berkeley. She was home for holidays and usually a month in the summers but this was the first time she had attended the company picnic with her family.

Sam told us, while we were cleaning up that evening, that when he saw Rachel it seemed like the world just stopped. She looked up at him and smiled and he felt light as a feather. Evidently, she felt pretty much the same about Sam. He called her the next day to see if she'd like to go to a movie in San Luis Obispo that evening. He said she didn't even hesitate but asked "What time will you pick me up? Do you know where I live?"

He assured her he knew and would be by at 6:45. She was ready.

Mitzi had made friends with many of the people at the party though she actually spent most of her time under the porch steps watching. But when Sam told her he was going to pick up Rachel and to a movie, Mitzi seemed to understand. She stayed on the front porch from the time he left until he returned—nearly midnight. Mitzi ran to meet Sam and Sam sat on the steps with his arm around the dog while he told her all about the evening. Woody said he couldn't help but overhear as he was in the living room and the front door was open. Apparently, the movie was never mentioned.

Sam was his old happy go-lucky self all summer. Rachel loved Sam and his dog. They spent a lot of time together that summer. This was her last year at Berkeley. Sam said he was seriously thinking of asking her to marry him. Ted and Woody suggested he do so before she went back to school but he thought it would be better to wait until she came home for the year-end holidays. He wanted her to have time to "process" him a bit before he got too serious.

I was surprised that he would jump into a relationship so quickly, especially after the Emily thing. But this seemed to be such a perfect fit. And because Rachel was as enthused as he, we thought it was a very good thing. I had always thought Emily was a bit of a gold-digger. Rachel was content just to be with Sam. He didn't have to buy her affections. He had long ago returned the ring he bought for Emily and now he was going to Morro Bay and San Luis Obispo to check out the jewelers. He wanted something different and said he'd know it when he saw it. Woody, Ted and I truly believed that if he had found "the" ring before Rachel returned to Berkeley, he would have popped the question. But he didn't find it before that she went back to school at the beginning of September.

Just before Thanksgiving 1944, Sam took me to the doctor's office for my annual check up. He said he wanted to do it because then we could shop for Thanksgiving dinner on the way home. After leaving the doctor we would try the new Safeway Store that had opened in San Luis Obispo. My, what a magnificent store. It made our community grocery look like a roadside stand.

There was a community bulletin board at the exit of the new store and I stopped to read some of the postings. I asked Sam if we could stop at this estate sale that was advertised for that day. The posting said rocking chairs and other furniture. I'd been wanting a new rocker, a smaller chair, than what I had at home. Sam said, "Sure. Why not? We're here anyhow."

The sale was only a few blocks from the store. It was mid-morning and quite a few people were there going through the things offered. There were many beautiful things including a small maple rocker. Exactly what I wanted. Sam was still driving his 1932 Ford and he said the trunk could hold the rocker, no problem. The rocker was in beautiful condition and it was only five dollars. While I was paying for the chair, Sam looked at the antique jewelry laid out on the table next to the cash box. Fine brooches, cameos, hair pins and a ring.

Sam picked up the ring and slipped it over the tip of his little finger so he could see it better. What a gorgeous ring; platinum old-fashioned filigree setting and a round diamond. The facets caught the sunlight and sent rainbows of color across the entire yard. It was, without a doubt, the most beautiful ring either of us had ever seen. Sam looked at it from every angle.

"What do you think, Mrs. Willoughby? Do you think Rachel would like this ring?"

The lady at the table said, "That was my grandmother's wedding ring. She and Grandfather were married in 1836 in Germany. The ring is about the only thing I have left of hers."

Sam wanted to know why she was selling it. "Well, I have no children and I don't want something so precious to be snatched by the State or some shrewd attorney after I'm gone."

The woman wasn't much older than I and I thought she was being a bit premature about dying. However, one never knows another person's problems. Sam slipped the ring off his finger and handed it to me. "Try it on, Mrs. Willoughby. Your hands are about the size of Rachel's. I want to see how it would look."

I slipped the ring on my left ring finger and held my hand out. The ring was alive. It was so incredible. Sam took in a deep breath. "How much is the ring?"

The woman looked at him, then at me and back at Sam. "$100. If you'd like to take it to Mr. Quince, the jeweler, to have it appraised, I'd trust you to do that."

Sam said, "I have to go to the bank. I don't carry that kind of money around." I slipped the ring off and handed it back to the woman. "Mrs. Willoughby, will you stay here and be sure she doesn't sell that ring to anyone else?" I nodded.

He picked up my rocking chair and put it in the trunk. He and Mitzi drove off to the bank. Mitzi went with Sam everywhere he went. She stayed in the car a lot of times as Sam didn't want to have trouble in places like the market. But she didn't seem to mind. Sam left the windows down and she sat in the passenger seat and watched people.

I talked with the woman while waiting for him to come back. She was delighted that the ring would be someone else's sentimental token. She asked about Sam and Rachel and, after I told her, she was sure the ring would be treasured. She told me of the hardships her grandparents had endured after emigrating to the United States. Her Grandmother had offered the ring as collateral many times but would never sell it. When her Grandmother died, her mother inherited the ring. She was sure that they both would be all right with her selling the ring to someone like Sam.

Not twenty minutes later Sam returned with two $50 bills. The woman put the ring into a small blue velvet ring box and handed it to him. "May your marriage be as blessed as my grandparents' marriage was." Sam thanked her profusely and we drove slowly back to Cayucos.

"You don't think I'm nuts, do you Mrs. Willoughby? The ring is exactly what I had in mind."

"No, Sam, I don't think you're nuts. I think the lady who sold it to you is nuts. That's a good-sized diamond. I think the platinum setting alone is worth the $100." I went on to tell him what the woman who had sold him the ring told me about it while he was at the bank. He was impressed that it was someone's family treasure.

Rachel was home for the Christmas holidays. She and Sam went to dinner Christmas Eve and then to a midnight church service. Sam asked her to marry him during dinner. She didn't hesitate but said, "Yes, absolutely." The ring was about a half size too big and, before Rachel left for school, they went to a jeweler to have it sized so that she could wear it.

That next evening at supper, Sam told us all about going to have the ring sized and what they had discovered about it.

The jeweler looked at the ring and asked Sam, "Is this a family heirloom?"

Sam replied that it was, though not his immediate family. The jeweler said, "I thought it must be. This is an incredible stone. The clarity and color are amazing and the setting must be early 1800s. No one takes this kind of care in a setting anymore." Then he said to Rachel, "You should really check into getting the ring insured. It's worth a great deal of money."

Sam asked, "How much money?" Sam had thought a hundred dollars was a lot. He nearly fainted when the jeweler told him he'd buy it from him right then for five thousand dollars.

Rachel said she was hesitant about wearing the ring. "What if I lose it?" Sam told her that's why they were here to have it sized to fit her finger perfectly. The jeweler said it'd be ready the next day. Sam said when they got to the car, Rachel bombarded him with questions. How could he afford such an extravagant ring? Whose family heirloom was it? Since they were in San Luis Obispo, he drove to the house where he had bought the ring. There was a "for sale" on the lawn. Sam spotted a man in a neighboring yard and inquired what had happened to the lady that had lived there. The neighbor said, "Oh, she died about a week or so ago. Did you know her?"

Sam explained he had bought something at an estate sale and had wanted to talk to her about it. The man said, "Well, it's too late now for complaints. Too bad your buyer's remorse didn't kick in a couple weeks ago."

Sam was going to explain that it wasn't remorse but decided it wasn't worth the effort. He got in the car and told Rachel how we had gone to an estate sale here, how I had purchased a small rocking chair and he bought the ring for a hundred dollars. He never imagined it was such a valuable ring but it was exactly what he'd been looking for to give her.

Rachel was overwhelmed. She said she didn't know if she should cry or laugh. Imagine a $5000 engagement ring! Sam told her that it was only fitting that a million dollar girl should have a five thousand dollar ring.

When he related that conversation to Woody, Woody said, "You wax poetic, Sam. Is this a new side of you?" We all laughed and finished supper. Sam was a bit embarrassed but soon got over it. Rachel had a week before she had to return to school. He said he'd be sure to bring her around so we could all see how beautiful the ring was on her finger.

I had known Sam all his life but had never seen him more content than at that very moment.

The winter moved right along. The weather was never super bad though we had a few heavy storms that just pounded the beach to death. Mitzi continued her habit of walking the Olengers to work but she came home afterwards and asked to be let in the house. At quitting time, she'd ask for out and go to meet them on schedule.

Some days I almost wished I owned a car. Walking against the wind and rain was hard. It was a very bitter winter.

In February Rachel called Sam one evening just as the Olenger men were sitting down for supper. I already had my coat on when the telephone rang. Rachel wanted to let Sam know that her application to teach in our local school district had been approved and she would begin teaching in the fall of 1945. Sam let out a whoop that she could have heard, without the telephone, clear down in Berkeley. His end of the conversation was interesting and I must admit I waited until he got off the phone to get her side of the conversation.

"That's great, Rachel. Are they paying you well?"

"No, of course, I don't care how much they pay you, I just don't want them taking advantage of you."

"I think that is a great idea. How about early August?"

"No, we could do July. I hadn't thought about a honeymoon."

"You pick out the date and let me know. I'll be there."

"Love you too. Thank you for calling with the good news."

"Thank you for that too."

Woody and Ted had gotten out of their seats at the table while Sam was talking. Mitzi had joined the circle and we were standing around like a group of vultures when he hung up. He looked at us and said, "What?"

Woody said, "You know what. Tell us what Rachel said."

Sam laughed. "She got the teaching job. The salary is pathetic but average. We are going to get married in July—right after my birthday. Rachel is going to figure out the date. She'll be finished with school in mid-May and will be home by the 20th. Anything else?"

Woody and Ted both shook his hand. They were so proud of Sam and marriage to a girl like Rachel was just frosting on the cake. I kissed him on the cheek and said, 'Be sure to invite us, Sam."

"Oh, Mrs. Willoughby, you all are my family. I wouldn't do anything as important as getting married if you weren't there." He gave me a hug. "You're all I have. And I love you all."

I brushed away a little tear . . . it was a happy tear. I hugged him and said goodnight. The three of them were chattering away when I walked out the door. It was an excitement for us to see Young Sam all grown up.

Over the next few weeks, Ted and Woody were debating what kind of wedding gift they should give to Sam and Rachel. They finally decided that they would talk to him and see if he wanted a house. One of the properties they had inherited was a small two-bedroom house about three blocks from the Olenger house. They had rented it out for a while but it had been empty for sometime. They would be delighted to fix it up, repaint it and give it as a wedding gift.

Sam thought it was a great idea and called Rachel to see what she thought. She was very excited about it. And so the three Olengers and Mitzi began spending time at the little house; repairing, painting and building a picket fence. By the time Rachel arrived home in May, the house was complete. Ted and Woody had the deed drawn up in both Sam and Rachel's names.

And by the end of May, it was ready for tenancy. When Rachel returned to Cayucos from Berkeley, she asked if it would be okay if she moved in before the wedding to finish up the little details. Ted and Woody pointed out that the deed made the house hers and Sam's so it was up to the two of them. Sam and Rachel began to gather furniture for the little home. Rachel parents helped her move into the house and her mother was there often to help make curtains and other things like that.

The wedding was scheduled for July 24th. The whole town was abuzz as Sam and Rachel were known and popular. Everyone in town would be invited.

But one afternoon Sam got home earlier than Ted and Woody. I was mixing biscuits at the counter. He sat on the kitchen stool, as he used to when a little boy.

"Mrs. Willoughby, I know you'll think I am just getting nerves but I've been having a dream lately. Like I used to have. The ones that always came true. I believe that I won't live to see my wedding day."

"Oh, Sam, maybe it is just nerves. You're healthy. What could possibly cause you to die?"

"I keep seeing a fire at the wharf. I don't know how but I know I don't survive it. My question is, do I say something to Rachel. I am so positive it's an omen."

"No, I wouldn't cloud her day in any way if I were you. It's been a long time since you've had dreams. It might just be nerves."

"I hope you're right. I really want to marry Rachel."

"And she really wants to marry you."

He hugged me. "I know. That's why this terrifies me so badly."

He watched me roll the dough, cut the biscuits out and put them on the baking sheet. "If something does happen to me, Mrs. Willoughby, will you help Rachel? Make sure she doesn't live alone for a long time?"

"It would be hard for me to convince her to marry someone else, Sam. She loves you so dearly."

"But will you be there for her?"

"Of course, Sam. If something happens to you, I will be there for Rachel until she doesn't need me. But I think maybe you're just getting last minute jitters."

"I hope you're right."

Ted and Woody came in just then and I put the biscuits in the oven. They kidded him about banker's hours as they all went to wash up for supper.

As I walked home that evening I wondered if Sam's powers were back. If they were, it was not a good sign. Sam's bad dreams always came true. Always.

Rachel planted rose bushes and a variety of other flowers around the house. Sam put up clothes lines for her in the back yard. Sam built a railing around the porch and then built a porch swing that hung from the porch ceiling. He and Rachel spent many hours in that swing in the evenings after their project for the day was done. Mitzi was always nearby one or the other of them. When Sam was at work, Mitzi spent her days with Rachel. She seemed delighted to have two special people to love.

Sam decided he should buy a suit to marry in as Rachel and her mother were sewing a very nice long wedding dress. Rachel's best friend was going to be her matron of honor and they were making her dress too. Sam said he didn't know it took so much time and effort to get married.

Chapter Thirteen

An unusual storm in mid-June caused several boats, in addition to the usual fishing trawlers, to tie up at the TWO dock. This had happened in the past but this time one ship was a large yacht full of unlikely sailors. Some big politico and his friends. The storm had passed but the yacht had not left. The passengers were all pretty much liquored up and Woody got the impression the crew was drinking as well. He didn't want to ask them to leave as drunken sailors on the sea are worse than drunken drivers on the highway.

Finally Ted spoke to the owner to ask when he thought everyone would be sobered up enough to leave the dock. The owner apologized and said that as soon as the cook had returned with provisions they were ready to cast off. He offered to pay Ted a daily rate for tying up the dock so long. Ted said that wasn't necessary but he would appreciate their earliest sober departure. The man insisted the crew was sober and not to worry; they would be leaving yet that day.

Sometime later the owner came into the office and gave the secretary a check for $500. He asked for a receipt and returned to the boat. Before she could notify either brother, or Sam, the yacht had gone.

I was up at the house and only heard about these transactions later. But for some reason Rachel said, telling us later, that shortly after noon that day Mitzi paced around the garden where she was working and suddenly took off in the general direction of the cannery. She thought that was very odd as Mitzi had never done that before but she also thought perhaps Mitzi had heard something she mistook for Sam's whistle or whatever. Rachel said she just went back to weeding.

It was June 18, 1945. I mention the date only because it is one I will never forget. The yacht returned. At full speed. It hit the dock. It appeared there was no one at the helm. People poured onto the wharf to see what the commotion was about. When the boat hit the dock, it rocked the entire building. The cannery line was in operation and the girls kept working while trying to see what was going on.

Woody went running to the yacht believing someone had to be aboard. After all when the yacht left the dock an hour before, there were four passengers and a crew of four. Just as he was about to step on the tilted deck, something exploded lifting Woody a good fifty feet into the air. He landed very hard. Fire scattered everywhere catching one wing of the cannery afire. There was massive chaos. Cannery girls were screaming—their exit was cut off. The blaze ran up the side of the building as though following a wick. I happened to be in the yard at the Olenger house and saw the fire erupt at the roof line. I ran down the hill to the cannery as quickly as I could.

There was no fire department in Cayucos but the secretary contacted many people to come help put out the fire. By this time it had spread to the loading side of the building. Sam ran in through the flames and got all of the cannery line girls out of the building. Someone yelled to him that Woody was down and he went running. Woody was lying, groggy and bloody, on the far end of the dock. Sam cradled Woody and asked if he thought anything was broken. Woody said no but he was very dazed and in quite a bit of pain. He was concerned that something internal had been ruptured as the pain was very severe in his mid section. He thought he had been hit by a flying mast from the yacht.

Sam continued to hold Woody until other help came. Woody said he would swear that as he was held by Sam, he could feel his insides coming back together. After Dr. Johnson arrived, Sam and Ted went back to the yacht. It was still afloat and most of the flames were out. They boarded and found the passengers locked in the main gallery. The crew had been tied up with duct tape; all the crew but the cook. Evidently the cook had gone berserk some ten miles out.

Sam and Ted were able to get everyone off the smoldering wreck except the cook whom they saw running about with a large knife. The yacht was definitely going down and Ted said to let the cook drown. It would serve him right. A call had been made to the County Sheriff and Ted felt he could handle the nut case—if the nut case got off the boat before it sank. To this day I cannot remember if the cook got off or not before the ship sank. I imagine that he did as I don't remember any to-do about it later.

Finally the fire in the cannery and on the wharf was under control. The bucket brigade saved most of the cannery but a large part of the inner dock was burned.

Sam was talking with the Sheriff when suddenly the large net unloading arm began to tilt from its position at the top of a mast positioned on the edge of the dock. Mitzi raced toward Sam, barking as she ran. But he didn't turn to hush her or see why she was barking. She ran into him full tilt hoping, I guess, that he'd move. If he had, the outcome might have been very different. But he was trying to outline to the Sheriff what had happened and ignored Mitzi totally. Something he had never done before.

The net arm fell slowly and rotated as it fell. It hit Sam from behind. He never saw it coming. Sam was dead at the scene.

Mitzi stood over him and howled. Everyone there that day says that was the most eerie sound they had ever heard. One they'll always remember. The dog was beside herself. She whimpered and nudged Sam's body. One of the work crew came and scooped her up to carry her away from Sam. Mitzi fought him but he refused to let her go until she calmed down. The dog appeared to be in agony.

The ambulance was ready to pull away with Woody when this happened and someone yelled to stop it. No one could believe Sam was dead and they insisted on loading his body into the ambulance next to Woody. The ambulance crew worked over Sam for several minutes and pronounced him dead. Woody was trying to get off the gurney he was on to get to Sam. He was delirious and obviously in pain. Ted crowded in and demanded that the ambulance leave immediately. He said later he felt he was losing the two people he loved most at one time.

Later on one of the rare occasions we talked about it, Woody said he is quite sure that Sam was in a weakened condition by having "helped" him earlier and so Woody blamed himself for Sam's death. I believe that Mitzi blamed herself for Sam's death as well. She disappeared off the wharf as the ambulance drove off. Someone thought she was following the vehicle but she wasn't. No one knew where Mitzi had gone.

Having run down the hill when I saw the fire I was on the dock at the time Sam was killed. After realizing he was truly dead, I called Rachel's mother. I told her what had happened and asked her to meet me at Rachel and Sam's house . . . the house Sam never lived in that Rachel had made into a home.

Rachel was delighted to see us coming up her front flagstone walkway. She and Mitzi came to greet us. I should not have been surprised to see the dog. It made good sense, when I thought about it, that when Mitzi lost Sam she would go to Rachel.

Rachel and Sam had just finished laying the flagstone walkway the previous Sunday afternoon. When she saw us up close and realized that we had both been crying, she clenched her mother's arm demanding to know what was wrong.

Her mother broke down into uncontrollable sobs. Rachel held her mother close; perhaps thinking it was her father. She looked at me. I choked up and after a few tries managed to say "There's been an accident at the wharf. Sam is dead."

The poor girl fainted dead away. She had such a tight grip on her mother it allowed her to slowly sink to the ground. Between us, we picked her up and took her inside and put her on the sofa. She roused a few minutes later and asked, "What happened? Tell me, what happened?""

Even after I managed to tell her, she could not believe it. She shook her head and said, "No, no, no. That can't be right. Did you see it happen yourself? Are you sure he's dead?"

Through tears I sobbed, "Yes, I saw it happen. Yes, I am sure he's dead." Rachel fell back on the sofa and began to cry uncontrollably. Mitzi nuzzled her arm and Rachel grabbed the dog and cried into her fur.

Her mother called the wharf to see if Dr. Johnson was still there. He was just leaving. There had been a few other minor injuries that he had stayed to patch up. She asked that they stop him and put him on the phone. When she told him who she was he said "Oh, my good god, I hadn't thought of Rachel. I'll be there in a few minutes. Who else is there with you?" She told him I was there and he replied, "Good."

The doctor arrived in a very short time. Rachel asked him, "Are you absolutely positive that Sam is dead?" The doctor assured her he was.

"I tried everything I could to bring him back. And Ted had worked on him before I got there. There is no doubt Sam is gone."

Rachel just crumpled into a heap. Dr. Johnson gave her an injection. He said it was a sedative that would wear off in a few hours. Meanwhile, he'd call a prescription to the pharmacy for something to help her through the next few days. Rachel's mother called the Wharf and asked for her husband. She asked him to go to the Pharmacy in San Luis Obispo to get the prescription Dr. Johnson was going to call in. He was in shock. He had just gotten home from his shift when the call came out for a bucket brigade at the wharf. Like Rachel, he refused to believe Sam was dead. He had seen him loaded into an ambulance. His wife had to be wrong. She was crying desperately and finally handed the telephone to me.

Rachel's father was surprised to hear my voice instead of his wife's. It seemed to shock him back to reality. "Good god, Agnes. It's true?"

"Yes, Roger, it's true." There was a long silence.

"I'll leave right now and be home as soon as I can. You're sure Sam is dead? Oh, my god, my baby."

An hour later I went back to the Olenger house without Mitzi. She refused to leave Rachel. Ted came in a few minutes later. The poor man looked as though he'd been wrung through a wringer. I asked how Woody was.

That started a flood of tears. He sobbed out that Woody would have died if it hadn't been for Sam. He's sure of it. Woody had a good deal of internal damage—a flying beam from the burning yacht had hit him mid-section and ruptured his spleen and liver and god only knew what else. But he was alive and would be tomorrow. Ted said that Woody was aware that Sam had been loaded into the ambulance with him and before he was sedated for surgery he kept asking how Sam was. I asked if he had told him.

Ted shook his head. "The doctors feel that he won't try to survive if he knows." He looked around and asked, "Where's Mitzi? I know she was there."

"She ran to Rachel. She's still there."

I took Ted into my arms as I would a small child and we stood in the kitchen together crying. It was the saddest day of my life. The little baby we had found nearly 22 years ago was gone. He was such a special child. He was such a good boy. He was such a wonderful man.

Finally Ted said, "So Rachel knows?"

I nodded. "She's an absolute wreck. Doctor Johnson has her sedated. Roger and Marge are in shock."

"Oh, Agnes, what do we do now?"

That question echoed through my very being for the next week. We decided to postpone Sam's funeral until Woody was out of the hospital. That was a long week. By then Rachel was functioning without sedation. Mitzi was spending all of her time with Rachel. When they were sure Woody would be home Rachel and Ted made the funeral arrangements for Sam. Woody was in a wheelchair. The wharf and cannery had been closed since the incident. The whole town was in mourning. I never realized how much impact Sam had had on people. Daily we heard new stories about Sam. Ted said he felt he should be writing them all down. It was unbelievable. But every story sounded so very much like Sam there was no doubt they were all true.

Sam was buried in his wedding suit on June 29, 1945.

There was no company picnic in 1945. The Wharf had been closed since the incident and no one had any heart for a picnic. But, unasked, all the workers showed up at the wharf on July 4th and began to clear the debris and charred timbers away. An insurance company had pulled out the yacht the week after the incident. The inner dock was totally repaired that Fourth of July. The net unloading arm had been totally dismantled. The workers said they could operate the old way. None of them wanted to see the thing that had killed Sam let alone operate it.

The wharf and cannery reopened a month later. Ted and Woody paid every employee for the full time of closure. I think it was one of the ways they felt they could honor Sam.

Over the next few months the cannery line that had been partially destroyed was rebuilt. And by Thanksgiving that year the wharf and cannery were back in full operation. Ted and Woody were mere shells of their former selves. They showed up at work every day and worked harder than anyone. All the employees were worried about them. Evidently Mitzi was concerned as well as she began showing up every morning to walk them to work and every evening to walk them home. But she was with Rachel the rest of the time.

Rachel started teaching as scheduled that fall. She was an excellent teacher and won a number of State Teacher awards in the next two years. She stayed in the little house she and Sam had so lovingly put together as their home. The deed was, after all, in both their names. Ted and Woody assumed she would stay and she did. After a few months she and Mitzi began to visit with them every Sunday. She asked if she could buy the deuce coupe that was Sam's pride and joy. They said no. They gave it to her.

After Rachel got the car, she and Mitzi took a drive to Los Osos one Sunday afternoon to the bird cliffs. Rachel said that Mitzi had been extra attentive to her that day. She thought it was because of the memories she had of that place. They returned home fairly late. When Rachel went to bed, Mitzi was on the rug next to her bed, as always.

The next morning, Mitzi was gone. Rachel made calls, put up posters, walked the beaches and the entire town—more than once. But Mitzi was gone as suddenly as she had come.

Mitzi's disappearance hit Ted and Woody almost as hard as it had Rachel. The three of them were like lost souls.

A year passed and things seemed fairly back to normal. The Olenger house was no longer filled with laughter though both Ted and Woody were functional. They looked forward to their Sundays with Rachel.

Late summer 1947, two years after Sam's death, Ted fell ill. He had no real symptoms; he just wasn't well. He became so frail and weak that Dr. Johnson put him in the hospital. Woody kept asking what was wrong with his brother. The medical community said they couldn't find anything wrong with him. He was just dying. Later Woody said it was a rerun of his father's death, after his mother had died. Ted died of a broken heart before September was over. Woody was devastated.

Before Thanksgiving 1948, Woody also passed away. Again, there was no physical reason. His will was read in early December. It was the same will that Woody had made before Sam tried to enlist in the Army in 1941. For some reason I thought they had all rewritten their wills. But they had not. And, then, all of a sudden, I owned the TWO Inc Wharf and Cannery, the big Olenger house and several other properties in town.

I closed up the big house.

Chapter Fourteen

Throughout 1949 I tried to decide what to do. It's an odd feeling to suddenly be wealthy. Woody had inherited from Sam and then from Ted. And now I had everything. I wanted to keep the wharf open but couldn't find a truly competent person to manage it. And what I knew about the business wouldn't have kept things going for more than a day. In June, I received an offer from a large cannery south of Cayucos. They wanted the name and the equipment. They had no interest in keeping the wharf and cannery open in Cayucos. I called a meeting of the employees and explained to them what the offer had been. They were crushed to think they would all be unemployed. I explained that some of them would be offered a position with the new company if they cared to relocate. Some of our equipment had been designed and made by Sam, Woody and Ted and the buying company would be interested in their working knowledge.

The meeting lasted for several hours. No one was bitter; no one was angry with me. Finally, they agreed it would be best if I sold the equipment and the name. I told them that I planned to give the ground the business sat on to the town. They offered to dismantle all the buildings after the equipment was gone. I told them that they could split up the materials, if they wanted to, between them. There would be lighting fixtures, office furniture, the furniture in the employee lounge.

I told them that after talking with the town, I had been asked to keep the office building intact. It had once stood alone and had facilities in it that would be useful for their intended use of the property. The employees agreed they'd dismantle everything except the original building.

Not one of them asked how much I was being offered or what I planned to do with the money. They were devastated that this long time landmark would be gone. I'm not sure they even thought about the fact I would be receiving cash for it. They did realize they'd be out of work but that never entered into our discussions or their decisions.

I suggested that as soon as papers were signed and the buildings vacated we should have one more meeting. There were 54 employees at that time. All had been there at least a year, many longer. They were agreeable; we could discuss actual plans then.

A month later I sent out word to meet at the wharf. The day before the meeting day, I went to the bank in San Luis Obispo with the certified check from the new owners of TWO Wharf & Cannery. It was for $756,000. I converted it into 54 cashier's checks of $14,000 each. There would be a few dollars paid later but I didn't know that at the time.

I wanted to do what I thought Ted and Woody would have done under similar circumstance. All 54 of the employees came to the meeting. I asked them if they still wanted to tear down the facility. I told them the town was excited about the gift of the property. There was an attorney working on the land transfer. Yes, they did want to tear down the buildings. I told them I had severance pay for them and began to hand out the envelopes. The first to open his looked at me with eyes wide open.

"Where did this much money come from, Mrs. W?" They all opened their envelopes then. So I told them that I took the proceeds of the sale, $756,000, and had the bank divide it by 54.

This was more than two year's salary for most of them. There were a lot of tears and muffled thanks. Now they'd have some breathing room while looking for another job.

A week later, everything but the original office building was gone—even the wharf. If you had never been to Cayucos before then you would never have known there was once a thriving business perched on the edge of the sand at the curve of the cove. I had many days of tears. My world had been stopped and restarted so often I wasn't sure if I was coming or going.

In August of that year Rachel came to visit me in my little house. She had met someone when she went to a Teachers' Conference the previous spring in San Francisco. He had just proposed marriage to her. She asked for a week to think about it saying there were so many things to consider. He didn't have a clue what had happened here in Cayucos and she wasn't sure she wanted to tell him.

All the time since Sam's death Rachel had worn the engagement ring he gave her. She wanted advice. She didn't feel it was right to keep it if she married someone else. We talked for several hours. We cried a lot of that time. Finally I suggested that she take the ring to a reputable jeweler and sell it. It would fund her new life. Sam would want that, I was sure. As she left she thanked me for my friendship all these years. She decided she should tell her new love about Sam and Cayucos and all that had happened here. She wanted to keep the house and I told her I thought Ted and Woody would approve of her renting it or keeping it as a vacation home or whatever she wanted to do with it. It had been her home for quite a while and there was no need for her to leave it until she was ready.

Later she called to say she had sold the ring for well over nine thousand dollars. I laughed and said, "Well, Sam sure knew a bargain when he saw one."

She sniffled and said, "Oh, Mrs. Willoughby, how can I love someone when he's dead?"

"I've done it for years, Rachel. I've never forgotten Mr. Willoughby. He was my first and only love. Someday, if you ever have the time and are curious, stop by and I'll tell you all about him."

Chapter Fifteen

January of the next year, I reopened the Olenger house. There were some minor repairs that needed to be tended to and some painting. I had a huge sale and sold nearly every single thing in the house. Sam's box of coastal debris, or whatever it should be called, caused many comments.

Many of the things in it were recognized. "Gosh, I lost that fifteen years ago." I heard a lot of comments like that and, of course, told the speaker he should take it. Some rock hound went through the box and took every one of the unusual rocks Sam had gathered over the years. It was an unusual sale in many ways. But I felt much better when everything was gone.

After the sale, I went through the Sears Roebuck catalogue and bought new furniture including a television, a washer and dryer. It was the first television I had ever owned. And I would never have to hang laundry again. Sears delivered everything in one large truck. It was an incredible day.

That was 1950. I've been here, in this house, ever since.

See what I mean? The one person I recall most vividly. What a simple question. But it was not told in an hour, was it? It's probably good the news reporter didn't press the issue. And I do believe that I will be here for at least another four years. Samuel Christian Olenger said so.

I think it's time to wash up my tea things and go to bed. Story telling is very tiring at my age. Too many memories. Just too many memories were disturbed to find that one special person I will never forget. Samuel Christian Olenger.